Wreck Me Again

Brit Easley

Wreck Me Again

Written by: Brit Easley

Published by: Sin&Spiral Publishing/ Brit Easley

Cover Design by: Brit Easley

Edited by: Brit Easley

Trigger Warning

This book is NOT a pretty little love story. It's messy. It's toxic. It's raw. It's anything but safe.

EXPLICIT 18+! (No exceptions!)

Ash and Sloane will wreck you, then heal you, just to wreck you all over again.

Inside you'll find:

Obsessive, love-you-then-hate-you relationships
Emotional manipulation & heartbreak that hurts
Cheating / infidelity
Alcohol & slight drug use
Profanity & very explicit sexual content
Violence, fights, and self-destructive choices
Mental health struggles
F/F Sexual Content
Toxic back and forth star-crossed lovers vibes
+ More

Ready to spiral? Buckle up, baby – you're in for one hell of a ride!

Don't Say You Weren't Warned!

...Now turn the damn page.

And prepare to be wrecked.

—Brit

Chapter 1

It wasn't supposed to be this way.

I wasn't supposed to fall in love with him—the one man who should've been untouchable. Off-limits. Forbidden.

Hell, that only made me want him more.

There was only one thing my twin brother ever asked of me after our parents died: Don't get wrapped up in *him*.

But here I am. Broken as fuck. Drenched in memories I can't erase because I refused to listen—to reason, to Colt, to my literal other half.

Colt has been saving me from myself for as long as I can remember. From fights. From grief. From the wreckage I can't stop hurling myself into. From my Borderline Personality Disorder and the bullshit that comes with it. He's the only one who's ever managed to pull me back, from anything—except from this. Except from *him*.

I never expected Colt to give his blessing. Or rather his okay. Because he damn sure didn't approve. He hated what we did to each other. But eventually, he didn't stop us anymore.

And with nothing to stop us... you'd think we'd have had our happy ending, right?

Wrong. So fucking wrong.

Ash Cameron Walker.

Just saying his name makes my blood boil and my chest ache. Fire and bourbon wrapped in barbed wire and chaos. Every damn thing I shouldn't want. And yet... I do.

He was no good for me. Wild. Destructive. Taking bad boy to a whole other level. And with him, my own recklessness knew no limits. I gave no fucks. Terrifying, really—the things I wouldn't do for him. Let's just say...*that didn't leave much.*

But dammit, the shit he made me feel... Things I didn't want to feel. Things I couldn't even begin to explain. Alive. Wild. Free. And in the middle of all that ruin, I felt unbreakable, too.

We weren't just fire and gasoline—we were an explosion on repeat, burning faster every time, leaving nothing behind but smoke. Every kiss was a battle. Every fight was foreplay. Every touch carried both devotion and damnation. A twisted game neither of us knew how to quit playing.

We loved like addicts; like every second without the other was withdrawal. But the high never lasted. Sooner or later, we'd crash, and when we did, it was brutal. Words became weapons. Touch became scars. And every time we swore it was the last... we'd crawl right back, begging for another hit.

I wrecked him, and he tore me apart. I'd push, he'd pull, and somewhere in the middle, we left pieces of ourselves scattered across years of chaos. Our love wasn't soft—it was jagged. Brutal. A slow-motion collision that left me dizzy and bleeding, begging for the next strike.

We didn't just destroy each other—we carved each other open and called it love—or something like it. And maybe that's what made it so addictive. Because nothing ever burned brighter than us, even when it left nothing but ash behind.

We should've walked away the first time. Or the second. Or the hundredth. But no matter how far I ran, he found me. Or I found him. We always ended up right back at each other, trapped in a never ending loop of deja vù we couldn't break.

The wreckage wasn't rules. It wasn't warnings. It wasn't the world.

It was us. Always us. Our reckless, stupid, burning desire to tear each other apart while pretending we could survive the blaze.

He's the ghost that lingers in every dark corner of my mind. That cocky grin. Those storm-grey eyes. The way he looked at me like I was all he'd ever need. And when I said there wasn't much I wouldn't do for him—I meant even if it destroyed me in the process.

He is my own personal torment. My own personal hell.

I feel him in every pulse of my veins. Hear him in the silence. See him in the shadows. He creeps in when I least expect it. Always there. Haunting me. *Still.*

He consumes me. Every thought. Every breath. Even in sleep, he's there—parading through my dreams like he owns me. *Because he fucking does.*

Being with him was dangerous. It was my undoing. It was my weakness. And in the end, it might very well be the death of me.

Because nothing hurt like Ash did. He could rip your heart out and make you thank him for it. Then leave you begging for more. Who the hell does that?

Yup. You guessed it. *Us.*

Some things you can't outrun, no matter how badly you want to forget. Some things claw at you from the inside, silent and relentless, tearing you to shreds. And some things? Some things never change.

And honestly? The only logical outcome to being with Ash Walker was my whole damn world up in flames.

I know this. But I'd still do it all over again.

Why? Because he lit something wild in me that made me feel invincible. Like I could conquer anything.

Anything... except him.

Every thought of him is a spark in my chest. Every memory is a wildfire I can't extinguish. He broke me, rebuilt me, then shattered me again—and somewhere in that chaos, somewhere in that ruin, I learned something terrifying: I would chase that motherfucker to the ends of forever.

I would let him destroy me. I would let him consume me. I would let him own me completely, even if it meant standing in the ashes of everything I once was. I'd let him make a mess out of everything I thought I had built.

Being with him... it was everything. Everything I didn't want—shouldn't want. Everything I couldn't resist. And somehow, the one thing I could never walk away from. He's the pull I'd never fight no matter how hard I tried.

Loving him meant knowing there is no happy ending for us in any sense of the way and still putting myself through the torment anyway. Why? Simple. Because I didn't know how to quit him.

Loving him wasn't just a choice. It was survival. It was surrender. It was everything I'd ever wanted and feared at the same time.

And the cruelest part? He wasn't just a part of my past—he was my present, and my future as well.

Because now... in just a few days, I'd be standing in my brother's house, my chest tightening with every breath, knowing he'd be just a few feet away. The same man who'd wrecked me once—or a hundred times over. The same man who'd never stopped haunting me.

I told myself I could survive it. I told myself it was just a wedding. But deep down, I knew the truth: nothing would survive me seeing him again.

Because Ash Walker didn't just own my past. He was about to claim every part of me I thought was safe. And there wasn't a damn thing I could do about it.

Chapter 2

The wedding has had me shook for weeks now. With each day looming closer, my anxiety sky rocketed.

But it's not like I could bail on my twin brother on his wedding day. He is literally my other half—my better half, at that. He's the only one that can tame the chaos in my head.

Colt is the only one that has ever understood me-even in my darkest moments. He's seen every one of them. All up until I moved to Cali and handled leaving Ash on my own. Hardest thing I could have done was what I did—not talking to my brother when I was so damn beside myself I didn't know what was reality or delusion. He let me have my distance when I left but I know it hurt him as much as it hurt me.

Colt and I, we've went through hell and back together. We had the perfect little life when we were kids. Perfect family, perfect house, perfect quiet little neighborhood. But when our parents died when we were six and our aunt and uncle couldn't take us because our uncle's health was deteriorating so we ended up in the foster care system.

From there we got moved around. Abusive foster homes, neglectful environments, dangerous situations. And Colt—God bless him—he was always saving me. From the bullshit life was throwing at us. It was never calm, never relaxing. We had to be in constant defense mode. Constantly ready for whatever fuckery was coming next.

Before we made it to the parents we have now, Shannon and Adeline-Quinn's parents, we were in a terrible neighborhood with the worst of the worst. Our foster parents were alcoholics that fought all the time. All of a sudden—a memory surfaced that I had buried way down deep in the darkest corners of my mind, in that very moment as a coping mechanism.

One night after a particularly bad fight between my foster parents, my foster mother had disappeared into the night, and my foster father was roaring drunk. I barely remember dinner that night—something in the food, maybe a pill he slipped in—because my head was heavy, my thoughts swimming in fog. Every sound felt distant, like I was underwater.

Then he came into my room. I remember the smell of beer, the anger, the edges of his face twisted, but everything else was blurry. My voice sounded far away as I screamed, but I couldn't make sense of the danger. I remember the shaking of my hands, my chest pounding, but nothing was real until I felt Colt's hand on my arm.

"Lo! Run!" he shouted, and suddenly I was moving, though I couldn't feel my legs properly. Shadows shifted, shapes collided, a lamp swung—someone fell—blood, maybe? I couldn't tell. I was floating through it all, half awake, half dreaming.

He pulled me down the stairs. I knew we were running, but I couldn't grasp how fast, where, or why. My thoughts slipped away before I could catch them. The night smelled like smoke and beer and something sharp, like fear itself.

When we made it to Ash's house two blocks away, my hands were shaking so hard I could barely knock. Ash opened the door, and I told him... something. I didn't even know if the words were mine. Then he was gone, and Colt followed him. I tried to see what was happening, but the world tilted, and I caught only flashes: fists, yelling, red lights bouncing across the walls.

Then there was the knock at the door that made my chest stop. Ash looked at Colt, and I felt some strange pull—but I couldn't make sense of it. He looked at me too, and my stomach dropped, even through the haze. He wasn't letting Colt take the fall. I knew that much.

Colt started toward the door. "I'll handle it—"

"The hell you will," Ash growled. His voice cut through the fog like a knife, sharp and dangerous, and final. "You need to stay with Sloane."

I wanted to move. I wanted to speak. But I couldn't. My body wasn't mine. My thoughts didn't form properly. All I could do was watch, fragmented images floating past—fighting, cops appearing, Ash in cuffs being hauled away, Colt holding me close. And then silence as he held me and I drifted off into blackness.

Years later, I'd remember none of the details clearly. Just flashes: their hands covered in blood, the sirens, the beating on the door, the pure dread I felt seeing Ash be hauled away. My mind had buried it deep, like a survival mechanism.

Colt holding me as our lives crashed out in front of us, the bond between us stronger than ever? THAT is exactly why I couldn't bail on him now.

After everything we've survived – after every scar and every night spent running from the bullshit – this wedding isn't just another day. It's proof we made it out of the hell we endured alive. Proof that maybe, just maybe, we finally get to breathe. That at least one of us get their happily ever after.

So yeah, I'm anxious as hell. My heart's in my throat, and my hands won't stop shaking, my nerves completely shot.

The thought of seeing Ash again, the whole reason I left my hometown–my home state, my brother, Quinn, and everything I ever knew, sent me reeling.

But bailing on Colt?
Not a damn chance. I wouldn't dare. I owed him so much in life.

He's been my hero since the moment we took our first breath – and even if my world falls apart all over again Saturday being in Ash's presence, I'll be at Colt's wedding. Because that's what twins do–that's what *we* do.

We show up. We have each other's back. No matter what.

Even when it hurts.
Especially when it hurts.

And *holy fuck* is this going to hurt.

Chapter 3

The way Ash had been cocky from the start was so exasperating, but yet so damn attractive at the same time. Instantly. Those dimples. That laugh that made my heart skip a beat. Oh, how I missed that laugh. But that laugh was trouble. That laugh was toxic. Everything about him was. And I knew it. But that didn't stop me.

I'll never forget the first time I saw him – that arrogant devil with the cocky grin that melted me every damn time. The pull was instant. And here's the kicker: we were seniors in high school still.

Colt had dragged me to a party at his friend Lena's house. I was scanning the crowded yard, trying to find someone I knew, when Colt had appeared beside me again after hunting Lena down, elbowing me lightly.

"Hey," he said, nodding toward the pool. "I want you to meet someone."

And then I saw him. Ash. About 6'2", leaning against his Harley just past the pool, drinking bourbon straight from the bottle. Chaos wrapped in muscle and leather. Faded ripped jeans, grease and oil stains. Dark hair a little messy – not in his face, long enough to curl slightly if wet.

Colt dragged me by my hand to where he stood. "Sloane, this is my new Underground buddy, Ash," he said.

Underground... the fighting ring Colt had started last year to bleed out his anger.

He looked up, and my world went sideways. Piercing grey blue eyes that stared straight into my soul. A scar above one eyebrow. He grinned at me, and my knees almost betrayed me on the spot.

"Sloane, huh?" he asked, voice low, laced with trouble. Holy fuck.

I nodded, mouth dry. "You heard him," I said, trying to sound playful.

"Oh, did I now?" Ash asked, almost like a challenge, winking. I could smell the whiskey on his breath.

He tilted the bottle toward me. "Want a sip?"

I hesitated for a heartbeat, then took it – because that's what you do when the devil offers something you know you shouldn't want. The bourbon burned all the way down, but it was his eyes on me that set my body on fire.

I shuddered, and he laughed. His laugh. Oh Lord. My knees weakened again, and that wink – that tiny, teasing tilt of his mouth – threatened to consume me entirely.

That's when I noticed it: the barbed wire tattoo curling around the side of his neck, sharp but faded, yet bold as hell. Like a warning.

He didn't look away. He didn't smile. Just watched me, like he already knew exactly what he was doing. His gaze alone electrified me.

Colt's grin faltered slightly. A flicker in his eyes – a warning, or maybe recognition – as if he could see the storm about to hit.

"Careful," Colt said, low and sharp, cutting through the haze like ice. He grabbed the bottle from my hand, rough enough to make me flinch. Not just about the bourbon – a subtle push to get me away from the pull I couldn't name.

Ash smirked, eyes never leaving mine. "Guess your brother doesn't think you can handle the burn," he said, mocking me.

Something inside me snapped at the challenge. My chest burned, not from the bourbon – but from the way Ash's gaze devoured me, hungry and relentless, like we were the only two people there.

"Please," I shot back, crossing my arms. "I can handle more than you think."

His grin widened, dimples cutting deep, and it damn near knocked the air out of me. He leaned in close, whiskey heavy on his breath.

"Oh, I don't doubt that, sweetheart. Question is—can you handle me?"

My pulse kicked, furious and reckless, but I refused to give him the satisfaction of seeing me fold. "Try me," I whispered, sharper than I meant to, a crack in my words betraying me.

The corner of his mouth tilted, dangerous and slow, gaze dropping to my lips for half a second – long enough to set my entire body on fire.

"That mouth of yours is gonna get you in trouble," he murmured, low and dangerous.

Colt's jaw flexed. "Enough. Let's go, Sloane." He grabbed my wrist, cold and final, dragging me across the yard toward our house.

"Not happening," Colt snapped, low and furious. "I saw the way you two looked at each other. Don't act like I didn't. No fuckin' way. Bad news, Sloane. He's nothing but bad news."

I opened my mouth, but Colt cut me off. "I've watched him play the fuck outta multiple women at the same time. All of them stuck on him. All at his beck and call. I refuse to let you be his next victim. He's bad news. Period."

I tried again. "Colt–"
"No," he slammed down harder. "Don't. Don't try to explain it away. I don't want to hear it. I won't let you ruin yourself over him."

Every time I tried again, he shut me down sharper, cutting, desperate. Eventually, I went quiet. My hand still stung from the way he'd yanked me out of that house, but what burned hotter was the fire Ash had already lit in me with just one look.

And deep down, I knew Colt was right. Ash was trouble.
But God help me—I already wanted more.

That was before the wreckage. Before the heartbreak. Before I learned what it meant to survive loving Ash Walker.

Now? I'm just trying not to bleed out every time I hear his name.

I didn't just leave Ash. I left me – the wild, reckless version of myself that only existed with him. The one who felt untouchable. Invincible. Alive.

It wasn't that I wanted to leave. God, I didn't. But I felt everything for Ash – too much. And I was scared. Scared of how deep he'd already cut me. Scared of how i ripped him wide open. Scared of what would be left of both of us if we seen each other again.

I knew we wouldn't survive it. So I ran... before we burned everything to the ground.

Chapter 4

My phone started ringing, pulling me out of my thoughts. I looked down, not wanting to answer it, but it was Colt. My twin. I knew why he was calling, and I couldn't avoid it anymore—especially with his wedding in just a few days.

I answered the phone slow and quietly "Hey C-Bear" and it wasn't a gentle greeting I got in return.

"Look Lo, I get why you left. I really do," Colt said, his voice calm but firm. "But you have to put the crazy away for my wedding. Because well... you know..Ash is my best man, so you two seeing each other is inevitable."

That damn word hit me like a punch. Every time it came to Ash, it made my chest ache.

"I'll be there," I said, trying to steady my voice. "Nothing—not even Ash—is keeping me from your wedding. Cage and I will be there."

"Sloane..." Colt said slowly, as if issuing a warning, "you know how messy that can get. Ash doesn't have a lick of common sense when it comes to you, and he sure as hell doesn't know when to zip it. You know exactly what you're setting yourself up for if you bring him."

I snapped. "It's been almost five years. He's over it by now. He's always had an easy way of replacing me anyway."

A sudden wave of sadness hit me—one I shouldn't have felt.

"But he hasn't, Sloane," Colt said.

That slammed into me like a ton of bricks. *He hasn't... after all these years... he hasn't moved on?*

And then my world stopped. My chest tightened, my head spun, my heart raced. Too many feelings, all at once, crashing over me. I could feel myself slipping—overstimulated, overwhelmed, on the edge of dissociation. My voice shook. My breathing caught. My body felt disconnected, like I was watching it happen from somewhere far away.

"Lo...just relax," Colt's voice cut through the chaos. "Calm. Breathe with me. You can do this. Sit down and focus. You're gonna be okay."

I sank to the edge of the bed, gripping the sheets like they were the only thing tethering me to reality. Colt guided me through steady, even breaths—in and out—until my racing mind began to slow, until my body felt like mine again. He always knew when I was losing myself in a spiral. Especially when it came to Ash.

"I've watched you survive Ash more than once, Lo," Colt said softly. "You're going to be okay."

I took a shaky breath. "Well... he knows Cage and I are getting married. Quinn accidentally told him."

Colt went quiet. Then, low and careful: "I didn't know he knew. This could get really ugly. You two better just... keep it together Saturday."

I drew in a deep, steadying breath. "I'm heading out in a couple hours. Love you... see you soon."

I hung up, heart still hammering. Keep it together. Easier said than done.

I was so royally fucked.

Because the second I thought of him—Ash Walker—my chest ached, and then I was twenty-three all over again. I couldn't stop the memory from surfacing.

"Meet me at our spot," he had said, voice quiet but impossible to ignore.

"You gonna ghost me like last time?" I snapped, hurt and betrayal lacing my words.

"You still haven't let that go? I told you I didn't ghost you. They picked me up, Sloane," he said softly.

I went silent.

"Come on, babe. Meet me at the old football field." His tone wasn't pleading, but it never had to be. I always went. No matter how pissed I was.

I walked clear across town to the abandoned field—bleachers worn and splintered, lights long dead, the place echoing with memories. This had been "our spot" for so many years.

And there he was, a blanket laid out in the middle, soft music humming from a portable speaker connected to his phone.

I collapsed beside him, laying my head on his chest. "Can you see that?" he whispered, pointing up at the star-studded sky.

"Look how bright the stars are tonight. There's the Milky Way," he said, tracing it out with his finger. We'd spent many nights here together and never had we seen the stars the way they were tonight.

"No way! I've never seen it before—only pictures," I breathed, listening to the steady thump of his heart under my ear.

"This is the first time I've seen it too," he murmured, pointing again. "There's Orion's Belt."

I gasped. "And the Big Dipper!"

"That's a beer can." he said laughing.

We traced every constellation, marveling at the sky, laughing and whispering, losing ourselves in each other. By the time we finally fell silent, we were wrapped together so tight, hearts syncing, falling asleep under the infinite night, entirely lost in each other.

And now, after nearly five years, I was supposed to walk into a wedding with him—Ash Walker—the first man I'd ever loved, standing just a few feet away as my brother-Ash's best friend- says his vovs. The thought twisted my stomach into knots.

I told myself it was just a wedding. Just a wedding. Nothing more.

But memories like the football field, the way his heartbeat had felt against mine, the endless night sky—it all came rushing back. And I knew, as much as I tried to brace myself, that seeing him Saturday would be like walking into hellfire all over again.

Chapter 5

I forced myself to pack for Colt's wedding, moving like a ghost through my apartment. My hands shook slightly as I folded clothes, tucking them into my suitcase with precision, trying to focus on anything besides the storm coiling in my chest. Cage walked in, arms sliding around me, warm and familiar. There he was—the man who'd asked me to be his wife. Two months engaged, a year together, and he had popped the question on our anniversary.

That night, standing on the balcony of his apartment, city lights spilling gold over us, he had that quiet, assured grin. I let myself believe it could be enough. Safe. Warm. Comfortable. For a moment, I thought maybe the storm inside me didn't need to rage anymore. Maybe I didn't need the fire. Maybe I could live without the chaos. Maybe I could finally rest.

Even wrapped in Cage's arms, feeling the warmth and safety, I felt the pull—the memory of fire and chaos I'd once lived for. The wreckage I couldn't forget. Safe wasn't dangerous. Safe didn't make me come alive. Safe was... just... safe.

That was Cage.
Safe.

Ash was the opposite of safe. He was reckless. Wild. The match I kept striking against my ribs just to watch myself burn. And even now—years later, with a ring on my finger and a man who would give me the world—Ash lived in me like an infection that never healed.

I should have been glowing. Excited. The kind of woman who gushed about venues and dresses and the future. Instead, I stood there with Cage's arms around me and felt... nothing. No fire. No spark. No chaos that made my chest ache or my pulse race. Just calm. Safe. Predictable. Comfortable.

But comfort doesn't set your blood on fire. It doesn't twist your stomach or make your brain buzz with desire. It doesn't haunt your dreams like Ash Walker did. Every quiet night with Cage felt like a gentle lullaby compared to the crackle of electricity I'd once shared with Ash.

I loved Cage—yes. Or maybe I convinced myself I did. But it was the kind of love I could walk away from. The kind of love that didn't anchor itself to my bones or burrow under my skin. The kind of love that wasn't dangerous.

We had nothing in common. He's a nightclub chain owner, buried in meetings or opening new bars. I'm a trauma therapist, always seeing clients, never home. I see him rarely, and when I do, it's like glimpsing another world I can't quite step into. He wants order. Structure. Predictability. I crave chaos. Fire. Movement that shakes me awake. Yet here I was, choosing the safe route, a route that didn't leave me raw and dizzy and wanting.

And yet, I stayed in a "safe" relationship. One that wasn't with Ash. One that wouldn't ruin me completely. One that didn't leave me aching the way he did.

Packing my bags, I folded each piece of clothing like I was sealing away a piece of my soul. Cage packed his, too, methodical and calm, humming some soft, forgettable tune.

Then together, we started the thirty-nine-hour drive from California to South Carolina. The highway stretched out before us, long and unyielding, and with every mile, I felt the weight in my chest grow heavier.

I rolled a few backwoods blunts before we left—because I already knew I wasn't going to sleep, and the thought of going home sober, of seeing Ash with all my walls stripped bare, was more than I could take. The smoke curled in lazy spirals around me, filling the car with a familiar haze, a temporary shield against the storm I could already feel waiting for me at the wedding.

This wedding I couldn't avoid.
To the moment I couldn't outrun.
To the place that would throw me straight back into Ash's orbit again.

The thought made my stomach twist. My pulse stuttered. My fingers tightened around the steering wheel as though I could steer myself away from what was coming. And yet... no matter how many miles I drove, no matter how many blunts I smoked, I couldn't escape him. He was there in the quiet hum of the tires against asphalt, in the rush of wind past the car windows, in every shadow and turn of the road.

I stared out the windshield, watching the trees blur past like the memories I couldn't keep from chasing me. The wedding wasn't just an event. It wasn't just a gathering of friends and family. It was a trigger, a countdown to standing face-to-face with the man who'd been my undoing for nearly two decades. The man who'd burned his name into my veins.

Cage squeezed my hand gently, breaking the tension for a fraction of a second. I turned to him, forcing a small smile. Safe. Warm. Predictable. And yet, in the pit of my stomach, I knew that no amount of safety could drown out what Ash had left behind.

I exhaled slowly, trying to convince myself this was just a drive. Just a wedding. Just... life. But the truth lingered, heavy and undeniable: Ash Walker didn't just live in my past. He was still here. Waiting. Pulling. Infecting every calm moment I tried to steal from myself.

And as the car hummed on, mile after mile, I realized the cruelest part of all: I couldn't outrun him.

Because sometimes, some things are just inevitable. Even when you know it'll be your absolute undoing.

Inevitable.
Ha.
How ironic.

Chapter 6

I had took the first shift of driving. I knew I wasn't going to be able to sleep anyway. Why bother?

Cage got comfy in the passenger seat, stretching out, his arm propped against the door as the highway stretched ahead—long, dark, endless.

The blunt I'd rolled earlier burned slow between my fingers, smoke curling out the cracked window into the night. The hum of the tires and the low music from my Spotify DJ blended into a kind of silence that felt too heavy, too full of all the things I didn't want to think about.

We drove like that for miles. Cage didn't ask what was on my mind. He never did. That was the thing about him—he knew when to press and when to keep quiet. Right now, I was grateful for the quiet, because my grip on the steering wheel was too tight, and we both knew why.

My mind was already a hundred miles ahead.

Home.

For Colt's wedding.

For the people I hadn't seen in years.

For Ash.

The name hit like a punch to the ribs—sharp, merciless, knocking the air from my lungs. I told myself it would be fine. I could smile, hug people, watch my brother marry the love of his life, and keep my heart right where it belonged—in one piece.

But the closer we got, the more I knew I was lying.

Because Ash was there.

And Ash was the one place I'd never truly left behind.

I had the music on low—just my Spotify DJ doing his thing, tossing out random tracks. Harmless background. But then he decided to ruin me. DJ can be a cruel motherfucker.

The opening notes cut like glass. My chest caved, breath locking tight. I knew that melody like I knew the taste of bourbon on Ash's tongue. Knew it because he'd put it there—years ago—on a playlist he made just for us.

My entire body went rigid.

That song.

Of course it had to be *that* song. Not just any song. *Our* song.

The one I hadn't heard in years. The one I'd avoided like it carried a virus, skipping it so many times the algorithm should've buried it in a shallow grave by now. But no—tonight, DJ decided to dig it up and carve me open.

It only took seconds before I was gone, pulled backward into a night I'd tried to forget.

We were stretched out on the football field, the damp grass sticking to the backs of my thighs. His Harley was parked on the edge, its metal still ticking as it cooled. The stars spilled wide and endless overhead, and Ash's arm was heavy around my stomach, anchoring me in place even as my chest buzzed with the urge to run.

"I made us a playlist." Ash said turning the portable Bluetooth speaker he brought with him on low. We listened to it for a long time while his arms were tight wrapped around me.

"This song especially reminds me of us." He said wrapping his arms around me tighter.

I traced the barbed wire tattoo snaking his neck, sliding my finger down the line of his chest. My voice was barely a whisper.

"You believe in fate?" I was looking into his eyes, drowning in the storm that was always brewing in them.

Ash tilted his head back, scanning the sky like he was daring it to answer.

"What, like the inevitable? The shit you can't control?"

"Yeah."

"I do," he said finally, low, carved in stone. His thumb brushed circles over my arm, slow and possessive. "But it doesn't mean what you think, Sloane. Doesn't mean we're written in the stars or some fairytale bullshit."

I blinked, chest tightening, heart hammering against its cage.
"Oh really? Because lying here with you feels... exactly like that."

He flinched—just barely—but I caught it. His jaw flexed, then he pulled back, creating an inch of space that hurt more than a mile.
"Sloane...it—"

"Don't." My voice cracked as I gripped his wrist, desperate. "Not tonight. Please. Just let me have this one night where you don't break me apart."

But his answer was a blade.
"I'm not doing this tonight."

My pulse hammered.
"Not doing this tonight? That's epic, Ash. You planned this whole night—you pulled me back into your bullshit, back into your fuckery—and now you're 'not doing this'?"

"I said I can't," he bit out, sitting up, dragging a hand down his face. "I'm not letting this—whatever the fuck this is—happen."

"'Whatever this is'?" My laugh cracked, sharp and mean. "Like you don't fucking know? Like you haven't been dragging me into this hell with you for years? What—are you scared? Scared to admit I'm the only

one who makes you lose control?"

His silence was worse than a scream. His eyes locked on mine, storm brewing even deeper, tortured, but his mouth stayed shut.

And that broke me.

"Fuck you," I snapped, shoving to my feet. My voice shook, but I didn't stop. "I'm done waiting for you to decide if I matter. Done letting you kiss me one minute and rip me apart the next. Done being the secret you only want when the world's asleep."

He stood too, voice raw, desperate.
"You can't walk away from me, Sloane! You know how this ends—every time. You can't, and I can't either. But if we don't—if we fucking don't—"

"I already have, Ash."

The words sliced me as much as they did him. I turned anyway. Legs shaking, forcing myself to walk.

I didn't look back—not even when his Harley roared alive and tore into the night like a threat, more so like a promise.

Back in the car, I blinked hard, holding back tears, shifting in my seat, trying to shake it off. My chest was tight. The past had teeth, and tonight it was sinking them deep.

Cage glanced over, brow raised.
"You okay?"

"Yeah." My voice sounded too light, too fake. "Just... tired."

He didn't call me on it. He just nodded and looked back out the window.

But we both knew the truth. He didn't know everything about Ash and I's history but he knew enough to know I wasn't okay. Not even a little bit.

In less than twenty-four hours, I'd have to see Ash again. And we both knew what that was going to do to me.

And nothing about that felt simple.

Not the first glance.
Not the first smile.
Not the way his storm-grey eyes would find mine in my brother's house.

I could already feel it–the pull, the ache, the wildfire waiting to ignite.

The closer we got to home, the heavier my chest grew. My hands gripped the wheel like it could keep me tethered, like it could keep me sane. But I knew better. No steering, no distance, no distraction could prepare me for what was coming.

Ash Walker. Just the thought of him made my stomach twist, made my blood hum, made me ache in ways I swore I'd never let anyone touch again.

And yet... I knew, deep in my bones, that seeing him again wasn't going to be something I could survive quietly. I'd feel it. Every pulse, every breath, every heartbeat would belong to him, whether I wanted it to or not.

I stole a glance at Cage, –safe, steady, not a care in the world beside me–and hated myself a little for it. I loved him, I told myself. I really did. But love wasn't going to save me.

Not tomorrow.
Not when Ash Walker was in the room.
Not when my entire world was about to explode.

Some fires can't be controlled.

And Saturday... I was walking straight back into the same damn flames.

Chapter 7

I looked at the man staring out the window, and my heart tugged. He was good to me. He loved me. He was calm. Safe.

But he wasn't Ash.

And we both knew it. He was the ghost we never spoke of. Even though he didn't know our entire history, but he knew enough.

My eyes lingered on Cage's profile as the miles ticked by, and the memory of how he came into my life crept in, uninvited, guilt running deep.

Three years. Three goddamn years since I walked away from Ash. Three years of clawing my way into some kind of life that didn't revolve around chaos and heartbreak. I'd poured myself into my work, into helping other people survive what I'd barely managed to recover from myself. I thought I was stronger. Thought I was free.

And then one night, a client dragged me too close to the wreckage again, ripped the scab off wounds I'd stitched closed with shaky hands. I was spiraling, desperate to get out of my own head, and so I stumbled into a bar that reeked of bourbon and bad decisions, praying a drink would burn the memories clean.

That's when I saw him.

Dark hair, tattoos inked like confessions across his arms, a grin sharp enough to cut me open. Trouble, wrapped in muscle and whiskey heat. I most definitely had a type. And God help me—I didn't even try to resist. My chest clenched, stomach twisting, pulse screaming "run"—but my legs carried me straight to the empty bar stool beside him.

He didn't speak at first. Just looked at me with a knowing that felt dangerous. Like he already recognized the ache in me, like he saw Ash's ghost tattooed across my skin and decided he could fight it for me. One look, and I was hooked.

Cage Lawson. That was his name. The sound of it felt like a lifeline, a promise I hadn't realized I was starving for.

"Dance with me," he said, grabbing my hand before my brain could remind me of all the ways this was a mistake.

And I let him.

God, I let him.

The music hit—slow, smoky, bourbon-soaked—and he pulled me onto the floor. The world blurred, the bar dissolved, and suddenly it was just me and him, spinning, laughing, colliding like gravity had lost its grip. Every brush of his fingers, every grin, every thud of my heart told me I was falling—not for him exactly, but for the escape he offered.

The lyrics wrapped around us like they were written just for that moment: "Round for round, 'til we're ready to leave, as long as you leave with me." My hands clung to him like he could erase everything before him, like I could press Ash out of my bloodstream by holding tighter.

The guitar riff surged, the words burned through me, and I sank into Cage like fire into oxygen. He wasn't Ash. That was exactly the point. He was anyone but Ash.

That night, I convinced myself I'd found my antidote. My safe place. My chance at forgetting.

And now, here he was. Sitting beside me. My fiancé. My knight in shining armor. My cure.

I looked over again. He had fallen asleep, chest rising steady and even in the dim glow of the dash. Safe. Calm. Predictable. The kind of man I could build a life with. The kind of man who would never haunt my dreams or twist my stomach into knots.

And yet... he still wasn't Ash.

I reached over and dug through my bag, pulling out another

backwoods I'd rolled. I hadn't planned on needing another one so soon, but the closer we got to South Carolina, the tighter my chest felt, and the louder Ash's ghost whispered from every corner of my mind.

I sparked it. Smoke curled into the car like a slow exhale. I leaned back in my seat. Cage slept on, oblivious, and for a moment, I envied him. I envied the calm he carried like armor, the way he had no idea what it was to be pulled apart by someone you loved and lost.

I inhaled deep, letting the sweet, earthy smoke fill my lungs, hoping it would take some of the tension, the dread, the sharp ache of anticipation with it.

The memory of that first night with Cage—the bar, the music, the way he'd pulled me out of myself, spinning me across the floor, letting me forget Ash even for a heartbeat—rolled through me. That night had been reckless, intoxicating, and freeing in a way that had scared me even as I surrendered to it. And now, sitting here, I realized just how much I'd relied on that reckless surrender.

I exhaled, smoke mixing with the hum of the highway, trying to convince myself that Saturday, like then, I could survive. That Cage could survive. That we could survive.

But deep down, I already knew.

Nothing could protect me from what was coming.

The inevitable.

Chapter 8

Raindrops began to splatter against the windshield—slow at first, then faster—streaking down the glass in jagged paths. The rhythm of it, the smell of damp air—it dragged me straight backward, no mercy.

The roar of his Harley under me. The pounding rain on our skin. The wind tearing through my hair. My arms locked around his waist as the world blurred into nothing but speed, sound, and him. God, the way it felt—like flying and falling and holding on for dear life, all at once. Both of us soaked to the bone. Reckless as fuck, drinking bourbon straight from the bottle.

Then he slowed, pulling off to the side of the road. I remember the crunch of gravel, the way my heart was still hammering when the engine cut off and the night wrapped around us.

He turned to me then, eyes dark and searching, like he was looking for answers he didn't want to find. He didn't touch me right away, just stared, memorizing me—like he knew this moment was going to matter.

I felt it too. We passed the bottle back and forth, taking swig after swig. The air between us was charged, thick with everything we weren't saying. And when his hand finally came up, fingers brushing a strand of hair from my face, my whole world tilted. One simple touch, and I was gone.

Ash tugged off his helmet, tossing it aside. Then he reached for mine, easing it free like he didn't want to break me in the process. His hands stayed there—cupping my jaw, thumbs brushing my cheeks, his eyes dark and burning under the dim wash of moonlight. He looked at me like he was about to confess a sin he had no intention of repenting for.

"Sloane," he rasped, voice gravel and heat. I swore he could say my name like a prayer and a curse at the same time.

And then he kissed me—hard. I could taste the bourbon on his breath. Not tentative, not testing. His mouth crashed into mine like he'd been waiting for this moment his entire life. His tongue pushed past my lips, hot metal dragging against mine—the flick of that tongue ring so sharp, so shocking, it sent me reeling. I gasped into him, and he swallowed the sound whole, groaning as his fingers tangled into my hair.

But he didn't stop there. He never did.

His hands slid lower, gripping my thighs, pulling me closer until I was straddling him right there on the Harley. The seat creaked under us, leather warm against my skin, and still it wasn't close enough. His palms were rough, greedy, roaming up the back of my shirt like he needed to touch every inch of me. The cool bite of his tongue ring against the roof of my mouth had me shivering, my nails digging into his shoulders, anchoring myself to him like the world might spin out without him there.

"Fuck, Sloane," he breathed against my lips, voice ragged. Tongue ring cold fire against my lips, licking, biting, leaving marks I knew I'd see tomorrow in the mirror. Each one felt like a claim, like he was stamping me as his—even though we both knew he couldn't keep me.

My head tilted back on instinct, giving him more, and he took it—sucking at the soft skin under my jaw, his hands sliding beneath the waistband of my jeans just enough to make me whimper. The night air was cold, but I was burning, every inch of me alive under his touch. My pulse was a war drum, my body begging for more, and he knew it. He felt it.

He pressed his forehead against mine again, breathless, sweat damp at his temple, his mouth hovering so close it hurt. "Tell me to stop," he whispered, voice almost broken. "Because if you don't..." His tongue ring dragged over my lip again, slow and deliberate. "...I won't."

And I didn't.

He dragged me closer, thighs gripping his hips, the Harley groaning beneath us. My jeans scraped against the leather seat, his hands gripping my ass so tight it bordered on pain, pulling me flush against the hard line of him. He ground up into me once, slow and deliberate, and I nearly came undone right there.

"Goddamn, baby," he muttered against my mouth before trailing down my jaw, tongue ring cold fire against my skin, then hot where he sucked and bit at my neck. Each mark he left felt like a brand, a claim. My head tilted back on instinct, and he took it—licking down to my collarbone, teeth scraping just enough to make me whimper.

I fumbled at his belt, desperate, clumsy, and he laughed into my skin—dark and low, like he loved seeing me lose control. But he helped me, tearing it loose, popping the button on his jeans, shoving them down just enough before his hands went for mine. He made quick work of my waistband, tugging me against him until there was nothing left between us but heat and want.

Then he was using his tongue ring, cool metal flicking the sensitive part of my clit over and over again until I squirted hard in his mouth and across his chest.

"Oh God, Sloane, I love how I can make you come undone."

And within a second, he was deep inside me. The first thrust stole the breath from my lungs. Raw. Deep. Reckless. I clutched at his shoulders, nails digging in, forehead pressed to his as we moved together, frantic and desperate, like we'd die if we stopped. His tongue ring flicked against mine when he kissed me again, the cool sting lost in the molten heat of his mouth, and I moaned into him, swallowing every broken sound he dragged from me.

The bike rocked beneath us, gravel crunching under the kickstand with each sharp movement, the night alive with the sound of his ragged groans and my breathless cries. I was unraveling fast, body sparking like a live wire, and he knew—of course he knew. One hand gripped my hip tight enough to bruise while the other tangled into my hair, yanking me closer as he fucked me like the world was ending.

"Oh, Sloane," he growled against my lips, guttural, breaking. "You'll always be mine."

Rain hammering down as lightning struck the sky and thunder crashed and echoed through the surrounding fields.

And I shattered. Right there on the side of the road, on the back of his Harley, under the unforgiving night sky. I came undone around him, clinging to him, biting down on his shoulder as wave after wave tore through me. He followed seconds later, growling my name like it was the only word he'd ever known, collapsing into me with his whole body shaking.

As the rain continued to pour down on us.

Back in the car, rain hammered harder now, drumming like the storm inside me. I gripped the wheel until my knuckles whitened, the Spotify DJ's cruel track still cutting through the air. Cage shifted in his sleep, oblivious.

The memory clung to me—sticky, burning, relentless. Every detail—the rain, the Harley, the taste of him, the claim of his hands—flooded back in a wave that left me trembling.

And then it hit me: in less than twelve hours, I'd be inside my brother's house. Facing him. Ash Walker.

I forced my eyes on the road, but I could already feel it—the pull, the wildfire, the ache.

The rain streaked the windshield, and in the streaks, I thought I saw his eyes. Grey. Piercing. Searching.

My chest seized, heart hammering like it could shatter my ribs.

And I realized, with a sick twist of dread and anticipation:
I was driving straight toward the only man who'd ever owned me—and I had no idea if I'd survive looking at him again.

Chapter 9

I hated myself for the memories I kept dragging up, each one cutting deeper than the last.

The sun was climbing, bleeding light over the trees, when my stomach finally betrayed me with a low growl. Cage caught it, smirking like he'd just caught me slipping.

"Breakfast, i gotta eat" I muttered, nodding toward the squat little diner with the flickering neon sign.

I pulled in without another word. We ordered greasy eggs, bacon, and pancakes to go. He teased me about drowning mine in syrup. I told him to shut up, shoved half the plate at him anyway, and he grinned like he'd won.

As we went to get back on the road, exhaustion hit me like a brick wall. The miles, the memories—they weighed heavier than my eyelids. I tossed him the keys. "You drive. I can't."

"Ok baby get some sleep," he said. Not a suggestion. An order.

And for once, I listened. Curled against the window, lulled by the hum of the tires, I let go.

When I stirred again, it was to gravel crunching beneath the tires. My heart was already racing before my eyes opened.

The house came into view. Familiar. Heavy. Colt's.

Cage slowed, throwing me a glance that said he already knew what this would do to me.

"You ready for this?"

I took a look in the visor mirror at myself. I looked rough. Like I hadn't slept in days. Like I had just wrecked my entire being for the last 39 hours. I fixed my hair and reapplied my eye liner and lip gloss with shaky hands.

The sight of that front porch hit harder than any punch I'd ever taken. Because it wasn't just Colt waiting behind that door. It was everything I'd left behind. And whether I was ready or not—coming back here meant Ash.

"Yes," I lied, hands still shaking.

I shoved the car door open before I could talk myself out of it. Morning air burned sharp in my lungs. Each step felt heavier than the last.

Before I could knock, the door swung open.

Colt. My brother, My protector. My other half.

Pressed white shirt. Sleeves rolled to his forearms. Hair combed back, golden-honey in the sunlight. Piercing green eyes—the exact shade I carried, only deeper somehow. Dimples flickered when he smiled, the same ones I had, only mine were pierced with dermals. Literally, he looked just like me, only in male form. My twin. My anchor. My best friend in life.

We just stared at each other for a minute. His eyes—my eyes, mirrored—held me still. Then his jaw flexed, and his voice cracked, just barely.

"Lo."
He's called me Lo since we were kids.

"Hey, C-Bear" I rasped, rough and uneven, because what else could I say; I've avoided this place like the plague.

He didn't hesitate. He pulled me into him, arms locking tight the way they did when we were kids. Like no matter how far I ran, he'd still catch me. My face pressed into his shoulder, and for a second it was too much—being back, being here, being home.

When he finally let go, his gaze sharpened, all steel and warning.

He leaned in close, voice low, meant for me alone.

"Keep it together, Lo, please . Yesterday's rehearsal was chaos enough—I don't need no crazy shit if you know what I mean."

His eyes flicked toward Cage, who stood a step behind me, quiet and steady.

"Hey," Colt said, casual but edged. Cage gave him a small nod. The tension in the air eased just enough for me to breathe.

Behind Colt, chaos buzzed through the house—voices overlapping, doors slamming, someone yelling about lost vows. Colt's wife Elise's laugh floated above it all, soft and bright, and a flash of her gown caught my eye. Even in the madness, she looked like magic.

I swallowed hard, nodded, pretended I could handle this. But deep in my bones, I knew the truth: keeping it together was the one thing I'd never been good at.

And then—like the universe couldn't resist twisting the knife—

I heard it.

That laugh.

Low. Rough. The one that used to curl around my spine and set every one of my nerves on fire.

Somewhere inside that house. Close enough that my pulse spiked, my chest locked, and my body betrayed me before I even saw his face, was Ash Walker.

Colt was still talking, still steadying me with that big-brother look. But I couldn't hear him anymore.

Because I was already drowning in that laugh.

Like my fiancé wasn't on my arm.
Like my brother wasn't right in front of me.

Like I haven't been gone for so long.

And then—my stomach flipped, my knees went weak, my whole world narrowed down to that damn sound.

And I knew, before I even saw him, that nothing would ever be the same.

Chapter 10

I walked into their beautiful house, every inch decorated like something out of a magazine—and it slammed into me all at once.

Music thumped. Laughter bounced. Glasses clinked. People moved like a tide I didn't belong in.

Cage stayed a step behind me, protective, steady. I barely noticed. My gaze swept the crowd, my heart hammering, every nerve on fire.

And then—I saw him.

Ash.

He wasn't across the room or tucked in some corner. No, he was right there in the middle of it all, talking to someone whose hand clung to his arm, laughing like the world was his and he owned every damn inch of it.

Our eyes met—and the effect was instantaneous. Insane. Nerve-racking.

My stomach flipped. My knees went weak. My chest cinched tight, like the barbed wire on his neck had wound itself around me.

It wasn't just a look.
It was history. Fire. Desire. Fury. Heartbreak. Obsession.
Two decades wrapped up in that look.

The air between us crackled.

Cage's hand on my elbow barely tethered me to the present. My vision tunneled, locked on that grin, that tilt of his head, that infuriating reminder that he still lived under my skin.

And then I saw her.

The woman leaning into him, laughing, her hand stroking his arm.

Not me.
Not the ghost of us.
Her.

My stomach dropped. Ash Walker had brought a plus-one—after Colt swore he hadn't moved on.

The world spun. My pulse thundered. My grip on Cage's arm was the only thing keeping me upright. Ash didn't move, didn't smile. Not yet. But the tension was deafening.

Then he smirked—dimples cutting deep—and my heart throbbed like it might explode. That pull between us—inevitable, electric, unstoppable—was still alive.

And it was coming.
That collision.
And there'd be no surviving it.

I tore my eyes away, throat dry as hell. But when I looked back, I froze.

It wasn't just anybody on his arm.

It was Ember. Fucking. Cole.

And she still had Ash's name tattooed on her goddamn neck.

The memory ripped through me like a cool autumns night breeze—

A *party years ago. Ember trying too hard, plastered to Ash like she belonged there.*

I lost my shit. Grabbed her by the hair and, with a snap of my fingers, had her on her ass.
"If you ever come near Ash again, I'll beat the holy hell out of you," I spat.

Later, storming out of the house, I'd caught a glimpse of her tattoo.

His name.
On her fucking neck.

It took everything I had not to beat that bitch black and blue right there. Colt told her she better get out of there before I could. And she did.

"I saw that bitch's tattoo, Ash!" I'd screamed, voice sharp, trembling with fury and disbelief as i walked away from him, him trailing behind me. "It's your goddamn name! You cant tell me there weren't feelings involved you lying fuck!"

"It wasn't like that, Sloane!" he shouted, chasing me into the night. "She... she was just a distraction... From you."

"The fuck outta here, Ash! Lie to someone who'll believe your bullshit! Cuz i aint the motherfuckin' one!"

I ran, Ash chasing after me, until we reached the abandoned building at the edge of town. Moonlight cut through broken windows, graffiti peeling, dust hanging in the air. Silence pressed down heavy.

"Sloane, don't—" He tried to grab my wrist.

I yanked away, rage and longing burning hotter than ever.

"Fuck you. I hate how you gave her a part of you like that. Part of you that was only meant for me! How fucking could you?!?!" Betrayal and pain cutting deep, my voice cracking.

"Sloane—" he reached for my hand and I pulled it away.

"And I hate how after all these years of denial...Trying to hide it, to ignore it, to bury it..in hopes it would go away...I'm in love with you Ash Walker...And I fucking hate you for it."

He went quiet, like trying to process the truth I had just spilled out for him. His grin was slow, dangerous, slowly spreading wider, eyes boring into me like he could see the ache under every breath I took.

"I always knew," he murmured, voice low, rough. "But I never expected you to say it."

In an instant, he closed the space, shoving me against the wall, bodies colliding. I didn't hesitate. My hands tangled in his hair, dragging his mouth to mine. His tongue pushed, claiming, and I gave back everything I'd been holding in. My nails dug into his chest, my body arching against his, desperate, reckless.

"You're so fucking full of yourself, Ash!" I gasped between kisses, shoving and pulling all at once.

He growled, low and possessive, pinning me harder to the wall.

"And you love it. You admitted it. You've wanted us for years. Don't deny it now, Sloane."

I couldn't. Every nerve screamed for him. My legs wrapped around his waist, pulling him closer, the heat between us impossible to ignore. His hands roamed, gripping, claiming.

"Ash... I—God, I need you," I gasped.

"And you'll have me," he rasped, dangerous, teasing. "Every fucking inch."

The abandoned building echoed with our chaos—our cries, our curses, our skin colliding. Every kiss was war. Every touch was surrender.

And in that moment—my heart beating out of my chest, lips bruised, tangled in fire—I knew the truth:
We had never been anything but destruction.
And I had never wanted it more.

The memory dissolved, but the rage, the ache, still clung to me. I hated that woman being a part of him back then, and I damn sure didn't like her being part of him now.

I was actually pissed and had no reason to be. He wasn't mine. I had no rights to him-no dibs at all. Hell I have a whole fiancé, for Christ's sake.

Every time I glanced up, his eyes were already there—locked on me, deliberate. Not casual. Not accidental. He wanted me to feel it.

And I did.
Lord, I did.

Ember leaned into him, whispering, laughing, her hand sliding higher up his arm. But Ash didn't look at her. Not once. His eyes stayed on me.

Cage shifted closer, brushing my back. "You good?" he murmured.

No. God, no. But I nodded anyway, because how the hell do you admit your entire body is unraveling under the weight of Ash Walker's stare?

The wedding started. Music swelled. The bride's hands trembled as she held my brother's hand. And I tried—I tried so fucking hard—to focus on anything but him.

But Ash—smirking, jaw set, eyes burning into me—made it impossible. Every time I looked up, his gaze was waiting, unflinching. Daring me to look away first.

I glued my eyes to the ceremony, to love spilling raw and real in the room. But my throat tightened with every twitch of his mouth, every ghost of a grin.

Even when Ember leaned in, whispering in his ear, he didn't look at her. Didn't smile at her.
He just kept looking at me.

By the time the reception hit, I was nothing but raw nerves and restless breath. Music pounded, lights flashed, bodies crowded the floor.

I should've been able to disappear into it.
But I couldn't. Because he was everywhere.

Ash danced with Ember, his hand at her waist, her hair tossing back as she laughed. But even with her body pressed to his, his eyes never left me. As I danced with Cage if I didn't *see* Ash staring at me the whole time, I *felt* him.

Every step he took felt calculated, circling, closing in. He didn't have to touch me. His stare was contact enough. And then some.

And every time our eyes collided, the air shifted—thick, electric, suffocating. And I swear everyone in the room felt it.

It wasn't just a look.
It was a promise.
A warning.
A threat.

And I knew—deep down—it was only a matter of time before he acted on it.

Chapter 11

The reception was chaos—music pounding, people laughing, bodies moving in a blur I couldn't breathe through. I needed air. Space. Anything.

I slipped down the hallway, heels clicking against tile, heart jackhammering. The bathroom was blessedly empty. I gripped the counter, staring at my reflection, willing myself to hold it together.

"Get a grip," I muttered, splashing cold water on my face. But my hands shook. My chest ached. That stare of his was still under my skin, crawling.

I opened the door.
And froze.

Because there he fucking was.

Leaning against the wall like he'd been waiting the whole damn time, with his sleeves rolled up showing tattoos crawling up and down his arms. *Those were new.*

Ash Cameron Walker.

The hallway was dim, the muffled thump of bass seeping through the walls. His arms were crossed, shoulders broad, tattoos curling beneath the cuff of his rolled-up sleeves. His gaze slid over me slow, deliberate, before locking onto mine.

"Four and a half years," he said, voice low, rough. "And you still look at me like that."

My pulse spiked, throat dry. "Move, Ash."

He didn't. He pushed off the wall, closing the distance, his presence swallowing the air around me.

"You think you can walk back into this town, into *my* world, and pretend like I don't exist?" His mouth curved, cruel and knowing. "Pretend like we never happened?"

"I'm not pretending," I shot back, though my voice betrayed me, trembling with fury—and something far worse.

His hand braced against the wall beside my head, caging me in. He leaned closer, close enough that I could smell bourbon, marijuana smoke, and his cologne that always made my knees weak. My lungs refused to work.

"You can lie to that poor bastard you're trying to move on with. You can lie to Colt. To yourself even," he whispered, breath ghosting my cheek, sending a violent shiver through me. "But not to me, Sloane."

I swallowed hard, glaring at him, desperate to hold my ground. "You've got Ember now. Go mindfuck her."

That smirk cut deep, dimples flashing like the devil himself. "Ember?" His eyes burned into mine. "Again...just like back on the day, she's a distraction. You're my goddamn addiction, Sloane."

My knees threatened to give out at the way he said my name. Every nerve screamed to run, to push him away—but my body betrayed me, leaning into the gravity of him, that pull I swore I'd buried years ago.

His lips hovered inches from mine, the tension so sharp it was unbearable.

And then—he stopped. Smirked. Whispered:

"Yep. That's what I thought. Still mine."

I shoved at his chest, voice low, shaking. "I'm engaged, Ash."

He caught my chin, tilting my face up until I had no choice but to meet his eyes. "It doesn't matter, Sloane. I'll always be in the back of your mind, no matter how many times you try to forget me." His finger traced over my lips, and my breath caught hard in my throat. "I could take you home with me right now if I really wanted to... and you wouldn't even try to stop me."

My pulse spiked. My heart pounded so loud I swore he could hear it over the music roaring from the reception—muffled but constant, like the world going on without us.

And I knew, standing there pinned between him and the wall, that this was only the beginning of the wreckage.

Before I could argue, Lena appeared around the corner like a hurricane with perfect timing.

Lena. Ash's best friend, sidekick, and faithful bike mechanic at Ash's shop, Walker Customs.

"I knew when I couldn't find you- where you were and what the hell you were doing, Ash," she said, voice sharp and dry. "So yours truly is here to save your ass before Colt finds y'all first. Not here. Not tonight." she warned.

Ash's eyes flicked to her, then back to me, dark and amused. He didn't move, didn't step back. But Lena didn't give a damn. She planted herself squarely between us, hands on her hips.

"You heard me," she said. "Both of you. Back to the reception."

The weight lifted just enough that I could breathe again, though my heart still thumped like it was trying to escape my chest. Ash's smirk never wavered, but for the first time in minutes, I felt like maybe—just maybe—I could survive this hallway.

And I knew, deep down, that Lena had saved us from immediate disaster—but she hadn't saved us from each other permanently. I mean, there's only so long you can detour the inevitable.

Chapter 12

The music hit me like a wall when I slipped back into the reception, trying to look like I hadn't just been pinned against drywall by the one man I'd sworn I'd never touch again. My pulse was still uneven, my skin still hot where his words clung to me like fire.

I plastered on a smile, grabbed a glass of champagne, and drained it in one go. Then another. If I couldn't kill the ache, maybe I could numb it instead.

Fake smile still in place—but it cracked the second I saw him again.

Ash, at the bar, glass in hand, Ember draped on his arm like she belonged there. He didn't touch her, not really. His eyes were on me, burning through the crowd until my skin lit up under the weight of it.

I laughed too loudly, let Cage spin me on the dance floor, knowing how insane it was driving Ash to see me in someone else's arms. I downed champagne until the room blurred. Every time I dared to glance his way, he was already watching. And every time, it gutted me all over again.

Colt appeared at my side eventually, hand steadying my elbow as I stumbled against him. His jaw was tight, his arm firm around me.

"You're done," he muttered, dragging me to the kitchen.

"I'm fine," I slurred, trying to wave him off. "It's a party—"

"It's a wedding," he cut in, sharp. "My wedding- at that. And you're not walking back in there like this." His eyes flicked across the room, lingering on Ash. His grip tightened. "Not when you're coming apart every time you look at each other."

The words hit me like a slap, but I didn't fight him when he led me outside. I couldn't. My body was too heavy, my chest too raw. And I knew he was right.

He lead me to Cage, who was already waiting in the truck for me.

“Keep her safe,” he warned Cage.

The ride was silent, except for the hum of the engine and my uneven breathing. Cage’s jaw was set tight, one hand clamped on the steering wheel, the other drumming restlessly against his thigh. I kept my eyes on the window, pretending the streak of headlights outside could drown out the way my chest still burned.

When the truck slowed, I blinked, squinting against the neon glow. The buzzing vacancy sign hit me like a punch to the gut.

No. Not here.

But it was.

That same shitty roadside motel. The one with the cracked ice machine and curtains that never closed all the way. The one Ash and I had used a hundred times when sneaking around was easier than breathing.

My stomach turned. *Motherfucker.*

“Why… why here?” My words slurred, but the question still burned.

Cage killed the engine, shoving the gearshift into park. “Because you’re drunk, Sloane, and you damn sure can’t stay at your brother’s with your state of unraveling. And I’m not heading back to Cali already—it’s been a long day, and I’m tired. We’ll crash here for the night.”

I laughed—bitter, broken. “Perfect. Of course we will.”

He didn’t hear the layers in it.

The lobby reeked of bleach and stale coffee, the plastic ficus still sitting in the same goddamn corner. Every step was a ghost. Every corner, a memory. The foreign guy at the desk gave us a keycard and Cage lead the way to our room, holding my hand to keep me steady. By the time he shoved the keycard into the door and led me inside, my pulse was a riot in my throat. Room thirteen.

Without thinking I blurted out "You've got to be fucking kidding me." Cage side-eyed me but didn't ask questions and for that I was so thankful.

The room hadn't changed. Same ugly floral bedspread. Same buzzing light above the mirror. Same suffocating familiarity.

I did not want to be here. I hated that I even came back. Even for Colt's damn wedding.

I staggered toward the bathroom, willing myself to sober up. I didn't have a choice. Either I pulled myself together or I was going to spiral completely. I felt disassociation coming on strong and with an unrelenting quickness.

I turned the bathroom sink on and splashed water on my face. I looked up at myself in the mirror. I had raccoon eyes from hell, eyeliner smeared from crying and wiping my face. I just stared at myself, self hatred and guilt running deep.

I did this. I ran five years ago. After he confessed his love for me. And then it was *me* who got engaged. I only have myself to blame for why Ember fucking Cole was on his arm tonight.

My gaze drifted from my own wrecked reflection to the cheap plastic frame of the mirror itself, my head still spinning. And that's when I saw it.

Just a tiny white corner, almost invisible, tucked between the mirror glass and the frame.

My breath hitched. Drunk and clumsy, I fumbled with it, my nails scraping against the glass as I tried to work it free. It was a blank Polaroid, faded at the edges. Taped to it was a small, square piece of motel stationery, folded tight.

My hands were shaking so hard I could barely open it. But I knew that jagged, angry handwriting.

You'll be back. Leave me proof.

I dropped it. The photo and note fluttered into the wet sink. I choked, a sound halfway between a sob and a laugh. The fuckin' arrogance. The *certainty.* The cocky bastard *knew.* He knew I couldn't stay away, and he'd left this–this game, this dare–waiting for me across five years.

I looked from the blank photo to my smeared, ruined face in the mirror, his words echoing in my head. *Leave me proof.*

I was here. I was back. But I was with Cage. The irony was so thick and cruel it stole the air from my lungs.

The spiral wasn't coming anymore; it was here, wrapping around my throat. I snatched the note and the photo, my heart hammering a wild, painful rhythm against my ribs. I shoved them back behind the mirror, deeper this time, hiding the evidence of a past that was still breathing, still waiting, and still, somehow, claiming me.

I splashed water on my face one more time and took a deep breath, trying to gain my composure but I knew it wouldn't be long and I'd be completely lost in myself and the ghost of him.

I opened the bathroom door and made my way clumsily toward the bed collapsing onto it with a dread that consumes me. I heels slip my heels off, the room tilting in drunken waves.

Ash's shadow filled every corner, thick and suffocating. The sound of his laugh here. The weight of his hands here. The way his mouth had stolen my sanity right there against the wall of my brother's house. And he hadn't even kissed me.

Cage tugged the blanket over me, his movements brusque but steady. "Sleep it off. You'll feel better in the morning. I'm going to shower."

Better.

Like anything about this could get better.

I stared at the ceiling, biting my lip hard enough to taste blood. Ash's voice echoed in my head, cruel and tender all at once.

Still mine.

The Polaroid picture with his cocky ass note attached. *You'll be back. Leave me proof.*

Unfuckingbelievable.

I wanted to scream. To claw the words out of me. To tell Cage the truth—that I was drowning in ghosts, that he'd brought me to the one place I swore I'd never come back to. The irony was too much at this point.

Instead, I turned my face toward the wall and whispered to no one:

"I fuckin' hate you, Ash Walker."

Nobody heard me.

But the walls did.

And if they could talk, boy, would they have some secrets to tell.

Chapter 13

I pressed my face into the pillow, trying to force sleep, but it wouldn't come. And then it hit me—the memory, jagged and alive, slicing through my skull like a blade. Our last night together. Our last night here.

My phone rang in the middle of the night. I knew the voice before I even looked.

"Come see me. I've got our room," Ash said. Stern. Demanding.

"Ash, it's two a.m.—besides, you could've called sooner. You've been home for days, and apparently I'm only worth a damn in the middle of the night," I snapped, trying to sound steady.

"Ain't ever stopped you before," he said. Those dimples, that cocky bastard's grin, crystal clear in my head.

Every nerve in me screamed. My body betrayed me—wanting him, craving him, the pull I could never resist.

"No, Ash—"

"Sloane, come see me. You know the room number." He cut me off. Definite. Demanding. Like my choice didn't exist.

Click. The dial tone.

Yep. I knew the room number. Thirteen.

I shook my head, pissed as hell. Three days since he'd gotten out of prison, and now—now he calls, middle of the night, same old game. And I'd go. I always went.

Rolling my eyes, muttering at my ridiculous self, I threw on one of Ash's shirts, grabbed my shoes and keys, and drove across town. Heart hammering, stomach twisting. Every red light felt like torture.

Ash was waiting at the door, cocky grin in place.

"I knew you'd come," he said as I climbed out of the car.

"Don't flatter yourself," I spat, pissed at myself for even showing up.

"I just couldn't sleep." Softer—like maybe he didn't realize how I'd flown over here like a bat out of hell.

Fuck. So long since I'd been near him, and every inch of me unraveled the second I saw him.

He kissed me hard, grabbed my hand, dragged me inside, closing the door behind us with a soft click that felt like it slammed against my chest.

"I want to show you something," he said, voice rough, pulling me toward the bedroom.

On the top shelf, a shoebox—heavy, worn, full of us. He flipped the lid, pulling out handfuls of paper. Every letter I'd ever sent: desperate, raw, pleading. Every scribble during his stints in prison, rehab, even basic training—proof of every moment I had bared my soul to him.

Then he dug deeper and pulled out more letters. Letters I didn't recognize. HIS letters back. Ink smudged, edges rough, gripped tight like they'd survived rage, regret, obsession, and the tiniest shred of hope.

He unfolded one. Voice low, clipped, trembling just enough to make it raw:

"I hated how you make me come undone. Like a damn wrecking ball no matter how hard I try to hold it together."

It hit my chest. Hard.

"I hate that I need you so bad I can barely breathe. But I sure as hell wasn't gonna admit it. Not to you. Not to anyone."

His jaw tightened. Eyes flicked to mine.

"You're the only time I lose all control. I hate how you wreck me, yet I come back for more. You consume me, and I let you. I can't stop it. And I fuckin' hate it!"

He was yelling now, the letter crumpled in his hands, voice raw, glistening with something almost like tears.

"I don't do safe. Never did. And I sure as hell don't do feelings—especially not for Sloane Carter. You're my goddamn kryptonite, but I'd rip my own heart out before I ever let you know that, before I ever give you that power over me."

He slammed the letter down, like it burned him.

"We tore each other apart because neither of us had the balls to let down our walls. Stubborn fools, that's what we were."

My chest tightened. Heart pounding. Tears stinging. But he just stood there, arms crossed, ego like a vault—untouchable, locked, impossible to crack.

"I'll never admit you're the reason I come undone. Nobody gets me the way you do. Nobody's seen me at my darkest. Nobody's done for me what you have. Nobody would ever dare."

"Your love hit different. I felt that shit from the start. And the way you never broke bad on me… you held me down. Every stint I've done, every broken promise, every heartbreak I caused…" He choked, looking me dead in the eye. "You're still here…"

"What I'm trying to tell you is…I'm in love with you Sloane Elory Carter" He closed the distance between us.

"Baby, I know it ain't pretty, but here's your truth. Our truth. This is our damn reality, babe. Embrace this shit."

He grinned, dimples lethal, eyes still wet. My knees almost buckled. My mouth hung open. Heart hammering so hard my head spun.

I just stared at him, eyes wide in disbelief. My mouth snapped shut, trembling so hard I had to sit down before I completely dissociated.

"Wh... why didn't you tell me before now?" I gasped, voice barely steady.

He knelt, grabbed my chin, tilting my face up until I had no choice but to meet those fierce, burning eyes.

"I'm telling you now, Sloane."

Fifteen years of silence. And here he was—finally confessing what we both knew deep down.

My chest heaved, panic and lust colliding, brain screaming run—but my body leaned in, betraying me.

Then he kissed me. And the years fell apart.

It wasn't gentle. His mouth crashed into mine, tongue ring sliding against mine, filthy, wet, consuming. He kissed me like he was trying to swallow me whole, like he'd tear me apart just to put me back together again.

Before I could catch a breath, he had me against the wall, one hand shoving my shirt up, rough fingers pinching my nipple until I gasped into his mouth.

"That sound—" he growled, biting my lip hard enough to taste blood, "—fuck, I've missed that sound."

His other hand yanked my panties down, elastic snapping as he shoved them off. I barely whimpered before his fingers were inside me—two, then three—stretching me open like I'd been waiting for him this whole time. Which I had.

"Dripping for me already," he snarled, curling his fingers until I cried out. "All this time I was away, and you're still this wet for me."

Shame and desire burned through me. I was soaked, clenching around him, every nerve screaming his name.

Then he dropped to his knees. His tongue was ruthless, relentless, dragging over my clit, sucking, licking, consuming me until my legs shook. His bruising hands held me in place, forcing me to take it, growling against me like a beast claiming his prey.

"Say my name," he demanded, tongue flicking, eyes dark. "Let me hear you break."

"Ash—fuck—Ash!" I screamed, shuddering against his face and against my will, completely coming undone.

He didn't wait. He was inside me a second later, slamming deep, thick, filling me so hard I couldn't hold back a scream. His hand circled my throat, stealing my breath while his hips punished me, claiming me in ways no one else ever could.

"You're mine," he snarled, pounding, voice raw. "Say it, baby. You're mine."

Tears blurred my vision, body writhing, overwhelmed by everything he was taking and everything I was giving back.

When the orgasm ripped through me, violent and consuming, I screamed his name like it was the only thing left in the world.

And when he finally claimed me—slow, deep, relentless—it wasn't just sex. It was every denied touch, every craving, every reckless, dangerous love we'd buried for years.

Exhausted, tangled together, it felt like we'd survived a storm, finding something fierce and unbreakable in the wreckage.

My head spun, body still on fire from the explosion between us.

Now Ash had every damn ability to wreck me in ways he never had before—and I knew he would.

I had to go. Had to run for my fuckin' life.

So I waited. Waited until his breathing slowed, until his arm went slack around me, until it was safe to move without waking the storm.

Then I slid out from under him, quiet as a ghost, every step a betrayal I couldn't take back. Guilt clawed at me with every move.

I went home. Packed my life into my car.

By six a.m., I was gone. California-bound. Leaving Ash Walker, my home state of South Carolina, and every piece of myself that still belonged to him in the rearview mirror.

I buried my head in the pillow, forcing myself to stop drowning in self-pity and guilt. Leaving ate at me in ways nobody could ever understand. And I fought myself for years after, to avoid returning home. Returning back to him. I ran from the only thing that ever made sense to me.

And still to this day...it's still the only thing that makes sense to me.

Chapter 14

The hum of the highway was steady, hypnotic. I leaned my forehead against the cool window, watching the blur of trees and headlights smear into streaks of color. Cage's truck ate up the miles beneath us, steady, reliable—just like him.

I wished I could feel that. Steady. Reliable. Anything except the cyclone ripping through my chest.

Instead, I let exhaustion do the work for me. Closed my eyes. Pretended if I slept hard enough, I could smother the memory of Ash—the motel, his mouth, his letters, the way he said my name like it belonged to him.

But sleep wasn't gentle.
Sleep was survival.

It came fast, dragging me under like a riptide. One second, I was clinging to the sound of the tires on asphalt; the next, I was gone, floating in that dark place where the lines between dream and memory blur.

I dreamed of his hands. His voice. That shoebox full of confessions I never asked for but always wanted. The wedding. *Still mine* playing over and over again. The way his eyes locked into mine.

I jerked awake once, heart slamming against my ribs, breath caught in my throat. Cage glanced over, concern flickering across his profile in the glow of the dash lights.

"You okay?" he asked softly, not prying, not pushing.

I forced a smile, the kind that didn't reach my eyes. "Yeah. Bad dream."

He nodded, believing me—or maybe just choosing to. Cage was good at that. At letting silence stand in for all the things I could never say.

I leaned back, tugged the blanket tighter around me, and drifted again.

This time, it was deeper. Dreamless. Black and blessedly empty.

When I woke again, the sun was bleeding pink and gold over the horizon. Cage was still driving, jaw set, eyes steady on the road. One hand on the wheel, the other resting casually on the console, close enough to touch if I dared.

For a moment, I just watched him. His calm. His quiet strength. The way he made everything feel safe even when I was chaos personified.

And yet—inside me was a fault line, still cracked wide open from Ash.

I sat up slowly, stretching the stiffness from my body. "Where are we?" My voice was hoarse, thick with sleep.

"Almost home," Cage said, glancing over with a small smile. "You've been out for hours. Thought about waking you, but... you looked like you needed it."

Needed it. God, if only he knew. If only he knew what I was really sleeping off.

"Thanks," I whispered, pulling my hair up into a messy knot just to give my hands something to do.

The truck fell quiet again, just the sound of tires on pavement and a country station humming low on the radio.

Life goes on.
That's the cruelest part.

You can burn alive one night, then wake up to coffee and laundry and errands like nothing ever happened. Like you didn't just sell your soul to the same devil you swore you'd never touch again.

I glanced out the window, watching familiar landmarks appear—

the faded gas station with the busted neon sign, the old barn on the corner with "GO TIGERS" painted on its roof, the crooked mailbox that had been leaning since I moved in four and a half years ago.

Home.

It should've felt like comfort. Instead, it pressed on my chest like a weight.

Cage pulled into the driveway, killed the engine, and turned to me. "You sure you're okay?"

I forced another smile, brittle as glass. "Yeah. Just need a shower. And maybe another twelve hours of sleep."

He chuckled softly, reaching out to squeeze my knee. Warm. Gentle. Anchoring. "Fair enough. You've had a long week."

A long life, I thought, but bit my tongue.

We got out, and I followed him inside, the scent of home wrapping around me—coffee grounds, clean laundry, Cage's cologne. Normalcy. Safety. Everything I should want.

I should've felt grateful. Loved. Enough.

But my chest still throbbed with the ghost of Ash's hands, his voice in my ear, his truth spilling like gasoline between us.

I dropped my bag in the corner, toed off my shoes, and collapsed onto the couch. Cage disappeared into the kitchen, humming low under his breath as he started the coffee.

Life goes on.
It always does.
But sometimes, it feels like it goes on without you.

I buried my face in a pillow, praying for sleep to take me again. To forget. To push Ash back into the shadows where he belonged.

But deep down, I knew the truth.

You can sleep off exhaustion.
You can sleep off hangovers.
Hell, you can even sleep off heartbreak for a little while.

But you can't sleep off Ash Walker.

And no matter how hard I tried, no matter how many nights I buried myself in work, silence, or Cage's steady arms, Ash was there. In my blood. In my bones. In the marrow of who I was.

Life went on. And I winged it.
But the storm was never really over.

Chapter 15

Life kept moving, even when I didn't want it to. That's the cruelest part. The world doesn't stop spinning just because your chest is caving in. The sun still rises, the coffee still brews, the clock still ticks, and people still expect you to show up. Smile. Pretend. Function.

So that's what I did.
Work. Cage. Repeat.

I floated through my days like some half-formed version of myself—not quite real, not quite present. Just... existing. I'd get up, shower, pour coffee I barely tasted, and drag myself into my office. My desk was clean, my degrees hung neatly on the wall, and the couch across from me was ready—waiting for someone else's pain to take up the space I refused to give my own.

It's funny, in a twisted way. I sat there, day after day, listening to clients unravel. Trauma. Loss. Betrayal. Abandonment. They poured out the things that kept them up at night, and I nodded, asked the right questions, gave them tools to breathe through it, to survive it.

They'd leave lighter. Calmer. Like maybe healing was possible.

And then the office would go quiet, and it was just me. Still drowning. Still bleeding. Still lying to myself that I wasn't a hypocrite.

Because I knew all the skills. I knew every technique, every grounding exercise, every step in the goddamn handbook. And none of it touched the part of me that still burned for Ash Walker. None of it rewired the way my chest caved every time I saw a motorcycle flash past me on the street. None of it silenced the nights I lay awake, aching for someone I had no business aching for.

And then there was Cage.

He tried, I'll give him that. He made me dinner sometimes, asked me how my day was, brushed his fingers over my hand like he thought maybe I'd soften if he just kept reminding me he was there. Sometimes, I let him pull me in, let him hold me while we watched some dumb show on TV. Other times, I'd curl away, blaming it on being tired, blaming it on headaches, blaming it on anything but the truth.

Because the truth was, he wasn't Ash.

And no matter how good Cage was, no matter how steady, no matter how much he deserved better than this broken-down version of me—he wasn't the man whose ghost haunted every corner of my life.

Nights were the worst. I'd lie awake next to Cage, listening to the rhythm of his breathing, wishing it was different. Wishing I could love him the way he deserved. Wishing I could erase the fire Ash lit inside me that never burned out. I'd stare at the ceiling and wonder if Ash was awake somewhere too. If he ever thought of me. If he hated me as much as I hated myself for still wanting him.

Sometimes, when Cage was asleep, I'd slip out of bed and sit in the kitchen in the dark, staring out the window like the night might hold answers. My phone always sat on the counter beside me. Silent. Empty. A black mirror reflecting back my pathetic hope. I never called him. I never texted. But God, I wanted to.

Quinn was my lifeline. She'd call sometimes—short, sharp conversations that felt like little gasps of oxygen in the drowning.

"You holding up?" she'd ask.
"Define 'holding,'" I'd joke, my voice brittle.

She never pushed too hard, never forced me to say the things I wasn't ready to. But she knew. She always knew. Quinn had been there for me in ways I couldn't even put into words, and sometimes I hated that too. Hated that she saw straight through me. Hated that she never let me drown quietly.

And then there was Colt. My twin. My other half. Our conversations were shorter. More careful. Like we were both walking a tightrope suspended over all the wreckage of our past.

"How's work?" he'd ask.
"Fine."
"You good?"
"Yeah. You?"
"Yeah."

That was usually it. Quick check-ins, like he was just making sure I was still breathing before backing away again. He didn't bring up Ash, and I didn't either. It was the unspoken law between us—never mention his name. It was safer that way.

But even in the silence, I knew Colt worried. I could hear it in his voice, the way he stretched out the pauses like he wanted to say more but couldn't. Maybe he didn't trust himself not to explode if the truth came spilling out. Maybe he just knew I wasn't strong enough to hear it. Either way, we danced around it, circling each other, pretending like everything was fine.

It wasn't.

Days bled into weeks. Weeks bled into months. I lost track of time, moving through life in this foggy in-between. I worked. I smiled when I had to. I let Cage kiss me, let him touch me, let him love me in the only way I could handle. Which wasn't love at all. It was survival.

Because if I stopped moving—if I let myself slow down long enough to feel—I'd crumble. And I couldn't afford to crumble. Not again.

Sometimes, though, memories slipped in when I wasn't careful enough. A client would describe the smell of rain before a crash, and I'd be twenty-three again, drenched on the back of his Harley, laughing through the thunder. A man's voice would crack in my office, low and raw, and it'd hit some part of me I'd locked away years ago. The smallest things dragged me back—like sucker punches, leaving me breathless in the middle of a session.

I'd ground myself. Push it down. Smile. Finish strong.

And then I'd drive home, my knuckles white on the steering wheel, wondering how much longer I could keep this up.

Then I'd torture myself awake with his words haunting me like the damn devil himself. *Still mine. I could take you home right now...and you wouldn't even try to stop me.*

Life goes on. That's what people say, like it's some kind of comfort. But they don't tell you how it goes on. How you can be walking and breathing and talking while feeling like you're already dead.

That's me. A ghost in my own skin. Going through the motions, smiling when people expect it, laughing when it's required, lying through my teeth every time someone asks if I'm okay.

And maybe that's what I deserve.
For walking away. For breaking us. For leaving him behind.

Maybe this half-life is the punishment.
Or maybe it's the only way to survive.

Chapter 16

I've always believed in signs.

Not in the cliché, horoscope-on-the-back-of-a-magazine way. I mean really believed. The universe doesn't screw around—it puts shit in your path for a reason. People. Songs. Accidents. Little nudges that feel too specific, too damn sharp, to be random.

I built my whole life on that belief. It's the only way I can make sense of the chaos. When Colt and I's parents died, when we got shoved into foster care, got abused, ect, when Ash came crashing into my life like a wildfire—there had to be a reason. Otherwise, it's all just cruelty. And I can't live in a world where things happen for nothing. Where nothing makes sense.

So I look for meaning in the mess.
Signs in the static. Beauty in the chaos.

And I swear, the universe has a twisted sense of humor.

A few months ago, on the way to Colt's wedding, I turned on Spotify DJ, let it shuffle me through its algorithm like it always does. And then that song came on.

Not just any song.
One of our songs.

I don't even know if Ash would remember it. Hell, maybe it wasn't even officially ours. But the second those chords hit, it felt like being sucker-punched straight in the chest.

I didn't act. I let it fade, shoved it behind the fog of the wedding, of work, of Cage, of surviving day by day like a ghost in my own life.

Same with the other instances where I convinced myself it was just coincidence.

Until today.

Today, the universe didn't whisper. It screamed.

I was driving home, sun lowering the world into streaks of gold and fire, Spotify DJ running through its playlist. And then—the song came.

Not a subtle nudge this time. Not a gentle tug. This song hit me like a tidal wave, every note vibrating in my bones. Every lyric was a direct line into my chest, a voice I couldn't deny. This was a song that didn't just play—it spoke. It told me where my heart was, what I already knew, and that it was time to follow it.

I gripped the steering wheel so hard my knuckles ached. My chest convulsed with a pull I could no longer ignore. My stomach dropped and twisted in that familiar, unbearable way. I felt every memory of him in an instant—the tilt of his head when he listened to music, the way he memorized every note, the fire in his eyes when he looked at me like I was the only thing in the world worth existing. The nights on the back of his Harley, screaming lyrics into the wind, chasing stars, chasing each other, chasing nothing but the raw chaos of being alive.

And the lyrics weren't just music. They were a command. A message carved into every fiber of me: you know where your heart is. It's time to follow it.

I parked in the driveway, hands trembling, chest pounding like it might burst through my ribs. Cage's truck sat beside mine, silent, safe, steady—the life I had built over the ashes of what used to burn. The golden light from the kitchen spilled across the driveway, warm and ordinary, and I felt like the universe was holding me at gunpoint, daring me to see it clearly.

The first song on my way to face him at Colt's wedding? That was a hint. A feather brushing against my consciousness, testing me, soft and tentative. The other small things I swore were random, also something that could be overlooked.

But this one? This was the universe yelling in bold, neon letters. This one was impossible to ignore. The push I'd been waiting for, the shove I'd tried to avoid, the hammer to the chest telling me I can't keep pretending my heart isn't where I know it is.

I let myself shiver. Let my chest ache. Let the memories wash over me like wildfire. For a few minutes, I didn't breathe. I didn't blink. I didn't move. I let it hit me in full force: Ash Walker isn't gone. He's not a memory I can tuck away neatly. He's written into me like a scar under my skin, a barbed wire brand that doesn't fade. He's the one I've been running from, but the universe is making it impossible to keep hiding anymore.

And yeah, I know what you're thinking. "You're being dramatic. It's just a song." But when you believe in signs like I do, it's never *just a song*. It's the universe smacking you upside the head. A cosmic reminder. A breadcrumb on the trail you've been trying like hell not to follow.

I felt it in my bones. Like it was written for that exact moment, for me, on that stretch of highway to the house my fiancé and I shared, with the sun dipping low and traffic crawling. It wasn't coincidence. It was a message.

And the worst part? I took it personally.

Because, of course I did. That's who I am. The girl who sees signs everywhere. The girl who takes a random shuffle on Spotify as divine intervention. The girl who convinces herself the universe is trying to tell her something–when really, maybe it's just a cruel reminder of what she's lost.

My throat ached from swallowing back tears I didn't want Cage to see later. My chest burned with that old ache I keep trying to bury.

And my brain–God, it wouldn't shut up.

What if it means something?
What if the universe is telling me to go back to Ash?
What if this is the sign I've been waiting for?

The kind of thoughts I spend every waking hour pushing down came rushing back in, uninvited, unstoppable. And for the first time in a long time, I didn't fight them. I leaned into them.

Isn't it funny how one simple song can flip a switch in your brain?

I couldn't make myself get out of the car.

Because stepping inside meant slipping back into the life I'd built on top of all the ashes. The safe, steady, quiet life. The one that doesn't burn me alive and doesn't set me free either.

And the universe was sitting shotgun, daring me to admit what I already knew.

That no matter how much time passes.
No matter how far I run.
Ash Walker is written into me.
Like the kind of love that doesn't fade—it just festers.

So yeah, maybe it was just a song. Maybe the algorithm had nothing better to throw at me in that moment. But I don't believe that. I can't.

I believe it was the universe reminding me that this story isn't finished. That ghosts don't haunt you without reason. That some connections are too raw, too carved into the marrow, to be buried alive. That some things are written in the stars and there's not a damn thing you can do about it.

It hurt like hell. It made me feel stupid and reckless and way too vulnerable for someone who should know better.

But for the first time in months, I felt something.

Not numb. Not ghostlike. Not half-asleep in my own skin.

Alive. Raw. Dangerous.

And isn't that what the universe does? It jolts you awake when you've been playing dead too long? It sends you songs that rip the scabs off, just to prove you're still bleeding.

I finally shut off the ignition, sat in the silence, and whispered to no one, “Okay. I hear you.”

The universe had spoken.
And I wasn’t sure if I wanted to listen.
I wasn't sure I was ready.

Chapter 17

I opened the car door, and the world felt heavier than it ever had. My chest was tight, my hands trembling. The pull in my heart wasn't just a whisper anymore—it was a screaming, insistent force, dragging me out of the life I had tried to build, the quiet safety I had tried to convince myself was enough.

Every step toward the house felt like walking through fire, every breath a reminder of what I was about to do.

I paused at the threshold, hand on the doorknob, heart hammering. Cage's laughter floated through the living room, easy and familiar, warm—the kind of life I had tried to convince myself could replace what I'd lost. He must be watching his show. And I almost turned away. Almost. Because leaving him, shattering him—it would feel like ripping out a piece of myself, too.

But I couldn't fight it. Not anymore.

I stepped inside.

Cage looked up from the couch, a smile lighting his face, and for a heartbeat, I almost wanted to melt into it, to let myself pretend everything was okay. Almost.

"I need to talk," I said, voice shaking before I could stop it.

He rose, concern knitting his brows. "You okay, Lo?"

I couldn't meet his eyes. I wanted to, but the truth was too heavy. Too raw. I let my gaze fall to the floor. My fingers twisted together, nails biting into palms. "No... I'm not. I'm... I can't do this anymore."

The words tore through me as I said them, raw and jagged, impossible to take back.

Cage froze. He didn't move at first, like he was waiting for me to clarify, to tell him it was a joke, that the tight knot in my chest was nothing. But he didn't.

"You... what?" His voice was low, steady, but it carried the weight of fear, of anticipation, and something else—pain, buried deep, waiting for me to confirm it.

"I can't do this anymore," I repeated, louder this time, forcing it out, letting it hang between us, thick and suffocating. "You deserve someone... someone who can love you the way you deserve. Not someone whose heart is... somewhere else. I'm sorry, Cage. I really am."

I finally looked up, and his face... oh, his face. Pain etched in every line, his jaw tight, but his eyes—softer than I deserved. He was devastated, but he wasn't angry. Not yet. Just... broken in the places I had caused. And I hated myself for it.

"I knew this was coming," he said, quiet, almost whispering. "After the wedding... the way the two of you were... there was no denying it. No matter how much I tried to ignore it, to pretend it wasn't true. I just... I couldn't be the one to break my own heart. I had to wait for you to decide this isn't what you want."

The words hit me like a punch to the gut. He *knew.* He understood. He had seen it. Even in my efforts to shield him, to bury myself in something safe, he had known. Always. He had always fuckin' known.

"I—" My throat tightened. I couldn't speak. I wanted to tell him it wasn't fair. I wanted to tell him it wasn't his fault. And it wasn't. But it didn't matter. The truth was, I couldn't stay. And we both knew it. Not when my heart belonged somewhere else. Not when my soul was tethered to someone who had left a mark too deep to erase.

He stepped closer, cautious, as if proximity might break us both further. "You've been trying to protect me," he said softly. "Trying to... keep me safe. From what? From him? From yourself?"

"From me," I whispered, voice breaking. "From us. From the chaos I bring. From the parts of me I can't... fix, can't control...can't heal. I thought... I thought I could do this. Be here. But every day, it's just... this ache. This constant ache I can't ignore."

Cage nodded, slow, deliberate. He didn't argue. Didn't beg. Didn't plead. He just... understood, in a way that made me feel both guilty and grateful at the same time. "You're honest with me," he said. "Even when it kills me."

I sank to the edge of the couch, hands over my face, trying not to cry. My body trembled, and the guilt clawed at me, sharp and relentless. "I don't want to hurt you. I never wanted to. But staying... would hurt both of us in ways we couldn't survive. I can't—Cage. I can't. Not when..." I trailed off, unable to say the words.

"Not when your heart is somewhere else," he finished for me. He wasn't angry. He wasn't bitter. Just... steady, wounded, accepting. And somehow, that made it worse.

"I love you," I whispered. "I just... not the way you deserve. Not enough to make this work. Not enough to stay where we know my heart isn't.."

He swallowed hard, jaw tightening. "I know. I know you love him. And I... I can't fight that. Not really. Not when you're already gone in your heart."

We sat in silence, the weight of it pressing down. The air thick, heavy with things we couldn't say. Things we couldn't fix. Things we couldn't take back.

"I want you to be happy," he said finally, voice low, steady. "Even if it's not with me. Even if it's with... him. You can't fight what's in your soul, Lo. And you shouldn't."

I shook my head, tears spilling down my cheeks. "I don't know how to stop being torn in half. How to... how to survive leaving you. Leaving us."

"You survive," he said softly. "Because you have to. Because life doesn't wait for anyone. And you... you follow your heart. Like you always do. You owe it to yourself, Lo."

The words were cruel in their clarity. My heart was screaming, my soul on fire, but I had to listen. I had to. I owed it to myself—and to Cage—to finally let go.

I hugged him then, one last time. Clung to him like the world was ending, like it was the last piece of safety I'd ever know. He didn't pull away. He let me. Let me hold on, knowing it was the last time.

"I'm sorry," I whispered against his chest. "I love you... I just... can't stay."

He kissed my temple, slow, deliberate, full of tenderness and regret. "I know," he said. "I always knew you'd have to follow him. And I... I get it. I hope you find your peace. Even if it's not with me."

I pulled away, tears streaming, heart breaking, lungs aching. I took my engagement ring off and placed it in Cage's hand, closing his hand around it.

"I'll send Colt for my things." I turned slowly toward the door, toward the night, toward the unknown. Toward the path my heart had always been begging me to follow but was now shattering into millions of pieces.

But for the first time in years, I allowed myself to step forward without looking back.

Chapter 18

Watching Sloane walk away was the second hardest thing I ever did, next to knowing her heart was with someone else.

I remember the night she first mentioned Ash Walker. It was a few days after we had first met.

We were on the beach, listening to the waves crash against the shore, underneath the moon. I asked her, "What brought you here to Cali?"

Her eyes went wide, like I'd hit a nerve she didn't mean to expose. She hesitated, swallowing hard before finally answering in a voice barely louder than the ocean. "I ran from a love I used to know."

I didn't push. I didn't ask who or why. I just sat there beside her, listening to the tide and holding her hand like maybe—just maybe—I could quiet whatever ghosts she was still drowning in.

After a long stretch of silence, she finally looked at me. The moonlight caught in her eyes, and for a second, I wished I hadn't asked. Her voice was soft when she spoke, but every word carried a weight I could feel deep in my chest.

"His name was Ash Walker. He's my twin brother's best friend."

She said it like it still burned her tongue, like the memory itself could tear her open. I didn't know the story, but I didn't have to—not when her voice cracked on his name. It wasn't just heartbreak I heard... it was history. The kind you don't come back from. The kind that never really lets you go.

"We were ruin," she said, her voice barely holding steady. "Nothing but destruction—annihliating each other every time we got too close. It was toxic, and heavy, and it hurt like fuckin' hell."

She took a shaky breath, eyes fixed on the dark horizon. "I had to run before he broke me into nothing. It was... too much. The kind of love that consumes you until there's nothing left to save. It was so intense it was terrifying."

I didn't know what to say. Every word she spoke cut through the night like glass, and I just sat there, watching the waves crash like they could drown out the sound of her heartbreak.

Jealousy burned somewhere deep inside me, ugly and silent, but beneath it was something worse—pity. Not the kind you give out of sympathy, but the kind that comes when you realize you'll never be the one someone runs to... only the one they run to to forget.

Her voice still echoed in my head—we were ruin. And I knew, right then, no matter what I did, I'd always be standing in the shadow of the man who broke her.

He wasn't brought up again until it came down to Colt's wedding. For weeks beforehand, she was nervous—distracted, anxious as hell. Didn't sleep for shit. Kept her distance. Hell, I was a damn wreck too.

"*Babe what's been on your mind lately?" I asked her as we ate our spaghetti, garlic bread, and salad for dinner one night. "I feel like your kind of distant lately." Her fork damn near suspended in the air on the way to her mouth. She snapped her mouth shut and put her fork down on her plate. "Colt's wedding is two weeks away..." She said quietly her voice becoming barely above a whisper. "Ash is his best man." She had finished, swallowing hard, eyes glassy holding back the tears with a quiet stubbornness.*

I will never forget the look of defeat on her face as I grabbed her hand across the table, giving it a little squeeze to reassure her. Why did I want to save her from him so fuckin' bad? Why did the thought of him ever having the chance to touch her heart again send a rage ripping through me? I shuddered at the thought, trying to steady my pulse from climbing.

"I'm sorry, Lo. I wish I knew what to say to make that easier for

you but I honestly don't know how I could make it any better." I said with a pain in my chest. My heart hurt.

"Cage... will you go with me?" She looked hopeful, eyes big with anticipation. I hesitated and before I could say a word she went on "I know it sounds crazy and you don't have to if you don't want to..." she said noticeably getting anxious at the thought of going back to her home state and everything she ran from.

"Lo, of course I will. Relax babe. I've got you. You ain't gotta face him alone."

I dreaded that wedding like I dreaded my end on this earth. I already knew what seeing Ash would do to her. There was no avoiding it. And I knew that if she saw him, that'd be all she wrote. There wouldn't be a place for me in her life after that.

I don't know what happened in South Carolina the short amount of time we were there, but when we got back home, she was like a zombie—barely functioning, like she'd left part of herself back there...back there with him.

As the days went on, I felt her slipping. I knew what was coming. I tried—God, I tried—with everything in me to keep her from drowning in him, but I couldn't. Her heart was still with the ghost of her past, and I could never be him. I could never fill the void he left behind.

Knowing where her heart truly was—that it wasn't with me, even after she agreed to marry me—was the hardest thing I've ever lived through. It wasn't watching her walk out that door after handing me my engagement ring back. It was knowing she'd been trying to prove she could love anybody but him.

She tried, I'll give her that, damn did she try. But the hold he had on her was too strong. I felt her slipping away. I knew it was just a matter of time before she realized she couldn't lie to herself anymore. I prepared for this moment even though it doesn't hurt any less.

As I heard her car start up and watched her back out of my drive, taking my heart with her, I knew from this night forward, I'd never be the same again. And I also knew deep down, I'd never love anybody else the way I loved Sloane Elory Carter.

Chapter 19

I had nothing but the clothes on my back, my car charger, and my purse—and I didn't even care.

The highway stretched on like it had no end, just black ribbon and headlights slicing the dark. My hands trembled on the wheel, knuckles white. The air in the car felt too thick, too tight, like it was choking me. My heart still throbbed with the echo of Cage's voice, that quiet resignation when I'd told him goodbye.

I couldn't hold it in anymore. My chest ached too badly. My stomach was in knots. I needed someone.

I hit Quinn's name on my phone.

She answered on the first ring. "Lo? It's late. What's going on?"

The second I heard her voice, the dam cracked. My throat closed up, words breaking on the way out. "Quinn—I left him. I left Cage and my heart hurts."

There was a beat of silence. Then, soft but steady: "Oh, Sloane..."

The tears came hot and fast, blurring the road. "I couldn't do it anymore. Cage deserves someone who can love him all the way, not just in pieces. And God, I tried, Quinn—I tried so damn hard to make it work. But my heart's not there. It's never been there." I was bawling now tears streaming down my face, uncontrolled, vision blurring as I tried to blink tears away to see.

"I know," she whispered, no judgment, no shock. Just truth. "I've known. I think Cage knew too. You've been half-here for months."

Her words gutted me, because they were true. I had been a ghost in my own life.

"Where are you now?" she asked.

I swiped at my face, sniffled, tried to steady my voice. "On the road. Heading back home."

Another pause, heavier this time. "To Ash?"

I swallowed hard. "To Colt. To you. To..." My voice faltered. "Yeah. To Ash."

Quinn exhaled like she'd been holding her breath for years. "Lo, listen to me. I'm not gonna tell you not to come home. I know you. Once your mind's made up, no one's changing it. But babe—be careful with him. With yourself. This isn't just another round of games. You come back here, it's gonna rip you wide open."

"I know," I whispered, voice breaking. "I feel like I'm already bleeding out."

"You're following your heart," she said gently. "And you've always believed the universe doesn't steer you wrong. So maybe this... maybe this is where you're supposed to be. Just promise me you'll call when you get close, okay? Don't make me hunt you down."

A weak laugh bubbled out of me, watery but real. "Are you kidding me? I need a place to stay." I said quietly.

"I got you. I'll get the guest room set up for you. Stay as long as you want" she said firmly. "Drive safe. And Lo?"

"Yeah?"

"I love you. No matter what shit storm you're about to walk into, I've got you."

The call ended, leaving me in the quiet hum of tires against asphalt. My heart still pounded, raw and aching, but Quinn's voice stayed with me—steady, grounding, reminding me I wasn't completely insane for doing this.

But as the miles slipped past, regret started whispering again, creeping in through the cracks.

Why was I doing this? Why was I running back to the man who had wrecked me time and time again? Why was I leaving safety, stability, someone who actually loved me, for chaos, heartbreak, unpredictability?

Because chaos was where my heart lived.

My phone buzzed. Colt this time.

"Lo?" His voice was low, calm—the way it always was when he knew I was barely holding on.

"Yeah. Hey."

"You driving? Quinn called me."

"Yeah, I figured. I'm a little ways out still."

He didn't ask. He already knew. He always knew. "I knew something was wrong. I could feel it. Be careful... we both know where things can end up with you coming back home..."

I swallowed hard, gripping the wheel tighter. "I know. I'm expecting it."

"I'll see you when you get here," he said, steady and simple. No judgment. No lecture. Just Colt.

I ended the call, and my stomach twisted tighter.

The closer I got, the heavier it felt. Every mile closer to home made my chest ache. My heart wanted Ash like it always had, but my brain screamed at me to turn the hell around. Regret tangled with excitement until I couldn't tell which was which anymore.

What if this was a mistake?

What if I was throwing my whole life away for someone who had never been safe, never been steady?

What if I was walking back into the same fire that had burned me alive before?

I pressed harder on the gas.

Because even if it destroyed me, even if I went up in flames, at least I'd be following my heart. At least I wouldn't always wonder what if.

And maybe, just maybe, this time the universe knew what the hell it was doing.

Chapter 20

I should've pulled over.

Should've closed my eyes for twenty minutes, caught a catnap before pushing further.

But I didn't.

I was wired.

Manic.

Riding the high of relief after unloading a guilt that had been strangling me for so damn long.

And the worst part?

It wasn't even relief over Cage.

It was the buzz of Ash Walker – just the idea of him seeping back into my veins, lighting me up like he always had.

It was chemical, I swear. Like those happy pheromones, endorphins, dopamine – whatever the hell science calls it when your body tricks you into thinking destruction is bliss.

I was on an Ash high.

My foot pressed harder on the gas, because my brain was drunk on him, my body craving that chaos. And then my mind did what it always does – rewound itself into old reels, playing back every other time I'd felt this rush.

The hum of the tires faded, swallowed by memory, and suddenly I was back there.

Back in that goddamn prison visiting room, where Ash sat across from me like a predator trapped in chains. Every muscle coiled, every dark thought blazing just beneath the surface, and I had known exactly how to push him over the edge.

I *wore that black shirt on purpose. Low, tight, dangerous. Every inch of me screamed "look at me," every movement–toss of hair, sway of hips, careless laugh—was a calculated spark. The guard's eyes lingered, but he didn't matter. Ash did. He was the one burning me up from across that table, already tasting me in his mind. Still didn't stop me from flirting with the guard just to watch Ash lose his mind. Which I did for a good few minutes. Until I was for sure Ash was going to break.*

Sliding into the seat, I pressed my chest to the edge, thighs brushing the hard surface, letting my gaze lock onto his. Dark. Hungry. Furious. The kind of look that promised destruction.

"You think that's funny?" His voice was low, ragged, a growl that made my pulse spike.

"Not funny," I whispered, leaning close to the glass, breath fogging it. "But watching you fight yourself...is pretty damn entertaining."

And then I let the words I'd been hoarding spill out, slow and deliberate, meant only for him.

"If this guard wasn't here..." My voice dipped into velvet, heavy with sin, "...I'd take you into my mouth, suck you dry, feel you shiver under me, and then I'd let you sprawl me across this table, lick me raw, my hot, throbbing pussy trembling under your touch. I'd let you bend me over, fuck me until every inmate in this bitch knows who's I am. Until your control shatters and every filthy part of you spills out inside me, mine to own."

His chest heaved. Knuckles white on the table. Eyes dark, desperate, on the brink of breaking. Every muscle taut like he could break the glass with a single thought.

"And then I'd scream your name," I whispered, reckless, shameless, pulse pounding, "so loud that it rips through these walls, so filthy and raw, everybody here would know it."

He leaned forward, the heat between us scorching, voice low and jagged, "Goddamn... Sloane you're asking for trouble."

I smiled, just a little. A smile that tasted like fire, sin, and desire.

"Maybe," I murmured, "but damn is it worth it to watch you squirm."

Even years later, my hands tighten on the steering wheel, thighs clenching, heat pooling low and fierce, and I can still see him exactly like that: undone, desperate, raw, and craving me.

If that guard hadn't been there? God help me… he wouldn't have just wanted me. He would've destroyed me. Right there. And I would've let him.

Every memory was a hit.
Every flash of him in my head another rush through my bloodstream.

I'd promised myself I wouldn't go back. I'd sworn I'd quit him cold turkey. But there I was, hurtling down the interstate, chasing my next fix like some love sick addict.

Chapter 21

I was stressing myself out wondering what the hell I was doing. With Borderline Personality Disorder, sometimes something makes perfect sense to you one minute causing you to make a drastic life changing decision, just to come back to your senses and realize how utterly and insanely stupid the decision you made was. Well this was my current mind state and I was spiraling hard.

At this point, I was full blown hating my irrational decision. Pissed as fuck that I left my calm, safe, stable life for a world of pain, regret and bullshit. *Make it make sense, Sloane.* But of course I didn't know how to. How do you make sense of the wreckage that I'm literally creating by coming back to South Carolina. By coming back *home.* By coming back for *him.*

I was halfway through town, listening to a playlist I shouldn't be because it puts me in my feelings, zoned out in thoughts of shit I'd rather never think of again—but still letting it consume me anyway.

All of him.
His name.
His voice.
The nights.
The fighting.
The fucking.
His cocky grin.
Those dimples.
The way him saying my name would make me throb.

It was after midnight when my phone lit up. I didn't want to answer, hesitating for half a second as my heart started beating in my throat—until I heard his voice when I answered after arguing with myself.

"Sloane."

Just my name, and that was all it took. My body betrayed me before my brain even had a chance to argue. Five minutes later, I was half-

dressed—nothing but a shirt and shoes—driving straight to his house like a reckless moth drawn to a flame.

By the time I got there, he was already waiting at the door. Arms crossed, mouth curved into that cocky, dangerous half-smirk with dimples cutting deep, that always promised ruin.

And then he said it again, low and wicked, like he'd been savoring this exact moment.

"Sloane."

My thighs clenched. My pulse roared in my ears. I hated how easy I was for him—how one word could make me ache everywhere all at once.

He yanked me inside, slammed me against the hallway wall, and his mouth was on mine before I could even breathe. Rough. Possessive. Claiming. His tongue slid over mine, and I gasped—metal pressed against me. That goddamn tongue ring, cold and sharp, teasing every nerve in me, sending shivers down my spine.

He groaned against my lips, pressing me harder, fingers digging into my hips, tilting my body against his. Every thrust of his tongue, every grind of that piercing had me moaning, trembling, losing control. I clawed at his shirt, at his shoulders, desperate for more, hating myself for needing it so damn badly.

He chuckled darkly against me. "God, Sloane… I don't even have to try," he rasped. "All I have to do is say your name."

And he wasn't wrong.
Cocky bastard.

Pissed at myself for even letting this memory surface—and even more pissed for letting my body remember it so vividly—I gripped the steering wheel, self-hatred spilling through me. Waves of sadness pressed against my chest, but I fought back the tears stinging my eyes.

Then I saw it.
Or so I thought.

I blinked, focusing, and yes—*I did see it.* A flash of chrome. The roar of an engine.

And *him.*

Cutting across the street on a blacked-out Harley, like he owned the goddamn road—like he owned me.

I slammed on the brakes, heart in my throat, hands shaking. He looked right at me.

I hadn't seen him but one time in five goddamn years. And still, he hadn't changed a bit—except for more ink covering that neck I wanted to strangle and worship at the same damn time.

Lord, why did more ink look good on him?!

Same broad shoulders in worn leather. Same short, messy hair I used to tug when he kissed me like he couldn't breathe without me. Same fucking eyes—wildfire and regret—locking on me like he'd been waiting the last five years for this exact moment. The moment I came back. Like he knew I would.

My foot still hovered on the brake. Heart pounding out of my chest. I forgot how to breathe. He always took my breath away. *Bastard.*

He slowed the bike—just slightly. Enough to look. Enough to see me.

And then he smirked.

He fucking smirked.

Like he knew I'd be back. Like he knew I couldn't stay away.

And then he was gone—just like that, whipping down Main Street, leaving my entire nervous system in shreds.

But I felt it. Every nerve. Every cell. Every part of me I'd tried to forget he ever touched.

On fire. Screaming. *Run.*

Ash fucking Walker.

Just my luck... the devil I had been avoiding for so long was the first to find me.

Chapter 22

I didn't even remember parking. Somewhere between Main Street and Quinn's door, I'd completely lost myself—disassociated. It had started getting dark when I had pulled into her driveway.

Even though I had come back because I couldn't let go of that ache inside me that only *he* created, I wasn't expecting him to be the very first thing I seen as I got to town. But then again, I guess that is just my luck.

My hands were shaking when Quinn opened the door, and she didn't even blink. Her blonde hair was tied in a messy knot on top of her head, sharp green eyes cutting through me like glass. Even in an old sweatshirt and bare feet, there was something effortlessly striking about her, the kind of beauty that didn't need polish.

"Oh no... Tell me you haven't already seen him," she said flatly, shutting the door behind me.

Quinn was waiting for me like I knew she would be.

I laughed—a forced, awkward laugh. More like a choke. Or, honestly? An overexcited walrus hyperventilating.

"Five goddamn years," I said, throwing my hands up, "and the first thing I see on Main Street is that arrogant bastard on his Harley, smirking like he owns my soul."

Without flinching, Quinn just said, "Of course it is."

She knows my spiral when it comes to Ash. She expects nothing less.

I dropped onto her couch as my knees betrayed me.

"He smirked, Quinn. He fuckin' smirked. Like he knew I'd be back. Like he's been waiting for the spiral."

"Because he has," she said, leaning against the counter. "That man has a sixth sense for mind fucking you—and you, for whatever goddamn reason, keep handing him the power to do so."

I groaned, sinking deeper into the couch. “I shouldn’t have come back, Quinn. I can already tell it's going to be a disaster.”

She didn’t even hesitate.

“Well, babe... some things you can't control. You left Cage and your life in Cali to come back home. And you didn't come home for Colt or I. And you know damn good and well that what’s meant to be will always find a way. And as much as I hate it—”

She paused, eyes softening despite herself. “You and Ash are inevitable.”

I groaned again, smacking my hand to my head. Quinn was right. We were one of those things.

I hated how right she was.

That five years, a state line, a thousand nights without him—none of it changed a damn thing.
Because the moment I saw him—just saw him—I was so royally fucked.

Quinn’s voice broke through my spiral.

“Guest room is ready for you. Get some sleep, babe... you’re gonna need it."

I nodded and headed to the guest room.
Right... like I’d be able to sleep.

Some ghosts don’t wait for night to haunt. Some hunt you down on Main Street, smirking like they never stopped haunting you to begin with.

The second I closed my eyes, the memory ambushed me—like it always does when I least want it. What came wasn't the parties, not the bourbon burn, not even the fights. No. What came for me was that night—the night he kissed me for the very first time.

It wasn't loud or wild. It wasn't one of our reckless explosions. It was worse than that.

Because it was quiet.
It was real.

We were eighteen, senior year of high school.

Colt had dragged me to one of his late-night football practices, swearing up and down he'd only be an hour. "Just wait in the bleachers," he'd told me. "Don't wander."

Of course, I wandered.

The night was humid, the kind that makes the grass stick to your sneakers and your hair cling to your neck. I was wandering along the edge of the field when I saw him—Ash. Sitting on the hood of his beat-up Harley, helmet beside him, head tipped back as he smoked.

The stadium lights had already been shut off. Just one flickering lamppost lit the parking lot, catching the sharp line of his jaw, the curve of that barbed wire tattoo like a warning scrawled in ink.

I don't even know what made me walk over. Maybe it was curiosity. Maybe it was that pull I'd been pretending I didn't feel since the first time I saw him. Maybe it was fate being a sadistic bitch.

He looked up when I got close, one brow lifting. "Lost, princess?"

I rolled my eyes, hugging my arms around myself. "Just waiting for Colt."

His smirk tugged. "Always waiting on Colt."

Something in his tone made my chest tighten. Like he was saying more than the words, like he knew exactly how much my twin had been my anchor through all of it—the foster homes, the chaos, the grief, the constant bullshit.

I should've walked away. Instead, I sat down on the hood of his bike beside him, pretending I wasn't hyperaware of how close our knees were, how his cologne and marijuana smoke curled into my lungs like a drug.

"You shouldn't smoke so much," I said.

"You shouldn't talk to me so much," he shot back, but his grin betrayed him.

We sat there in silence for a while, the cicadas buzzing, the distant sound of Colt yelling plays from across the field echoing faintly. And then Ash spoke again, quieter this time.

"You ever feel like you're alive... but not really living?"

The question hit me like a punch. My throat closed, because yes. Yes, I did.

I nodded, and for once, I didn't cover it with sarcasm. "All the time."

He studied me then—really studied me. Like I wasn't Colt's sister, like I wasn't off-limits, like I wasn't just some girl he was killing time with.

His eyes softened, dark and searching, and suddenly the whole world narrowed to just that moment.

I felt it before it happened. The charge in the air, the pull in my chest. My heart was a drum in my ribcage, my hands clammy, my breath shallow.

And then he leaned in.

Slow. Careful. Like he was giving me time to stop him.

I didn't.

The first brush of his lips against mine was tentative—testing. Just a whisper of a kiss, feather-light, gone before it even started. But it lit something inside me I didn't even know existed.

He pulled back slightly, searching my face. "Sloane..."

"Do it again," I whispered, before I could think.

His mouth curved into the faintest grin. And then he kissed me again—this time with intent.

It wasn't soft anymore. It was heat and hunger, the kind of kiss that steals the air straight from your lungs. His hand slid into my hair, tilting my head, pulling me deeper until I melted against him. My fingers curled into his shirt, desperate to anchor myself to something, anything, because I was spinning.

The world disappeared. The cicadas, the field, even Colt's voice in the distance—it all vanished. There was only his mouth on mine, his breath mixing with mine, his heartbeat pounding against me as if it belonged there.

And I knew—God help me, I knew—this wasn't just a kiss.

This was the line. The one we weren't supposed to cross. The one we could never uncross once it was done.

When he finally pulled back, I was dizzy, lips swollen, chest aching. He rested his forehead against mine, eyes closed like he was trying to catch his breath too.

"You know this is a mistake," he murmured.

I laughed softly, breathless. "Without a doubt. Biggest one I'll ever make."

His lips brushed mine one more time, quick and desperate, before he pulled away completely. He lit a blunt, hands shaking just enough that I noticed.

"Don't tell Colt," he said.

"As if I would."

We sat there in silence again, but nothing about it was the same. Something fundamental had shifted. A match had been struck, and no amount of denial would ever smother it again.

And lying there in Quinn's apartment now, years later, I could still feel it—the warmth of his lips, the way his hand tangled in my hair, the dizzying rush of knowing I'd just ruined myself forever.

My first kiss wasn't sweet. It wasn't innocent. It was doomed from the fucking start.

My mind was plummeting. Memories taking over.
My heart? Aching.
For the wreckage. For the inevitable. For Ash fuckin' Walker.

Chapter 23

Oil, burnt rubber, sweat, and dust—yeah, my favorite kind of perfume. I was half under a bike, elbow-deep in grease, when I heard it over my music playing on the speaker.

Ash stormed into Walker Customs like a goddamn bomb going off, steel door slamming behind him so hard the walls rattled.

"Motherf—" I grumbled, smacking my head on the undercarriage before rolling out.

And there he was.
Ash Walker.
Face red, veins bulging, chaos wrapped in leather, rage, and something I couldn't quite place yet.

I leaned on my wrench, cocked a brow. "You look like you just saw a ghost."

He didn't answer. Didn't even blink. Just stormed straight to the punching bag in the corner and tore into it like the damn world owed him blood.

Leather cracked under his fists, every hit harder than the last. Breath ragged. Shoulders tight. The sound echoed off the concrete—familiar, too familiar.

Oh no.

I didn't need to ask.

I'd seen this movie before—too many times. On repeat. For the last two decades. My breath caught.

Every time he came apart, it was the same rhythm, the same

tremor in his hands, the same name muttered under his breath like poison he couldn't get enough of.

And then he said it.
"Sloane's back."

Two words. That's all it took to make the whole damn shop stop breathing. My chest ached. My pulse quickened. And I was fuckin' pissed. *How dare she.*

He froze, fists pressed to the bag, head down, chest heaving. The man who could stare down anyone, throw a punch without blinking, never sheds a tear—broken into shambles. And I knew with every part of me that it was only going to get worse.

I swallowed hard, trying to hold it together. Trying not to think of all the progress I'd made with him, trying to put him back together over her. All for her to waltz back in like she didn't ever rip his heart out, and undo everything I had spent years doing.

Goddamn you, Sloane Carter.

Memories flashed. The bar fight. That idiot who dared smile at her. Ash dragging him outside and beat him till his knuckles split. Me using every ounce of strength and energy to pull him off of the poor guy.

Then coming here, to the shop, destroying that same spot, different punching bag until I thought he'd tear the bolts out of the ceiling. He had to replace it the next day. It was completely shredded.

The hours after—me bandaging him up while he reeked of whiskey and regret, muttering that he couldn't forget her no matter how hard he tried.

He'd spiraled before. Hell, I'd watched him drown in it—drunk, reckless, fists and fury and one-night stands that meant nothing. He only ever got that way when it came to Sloane, or lack of, I guess I should say. And now? Here we were again. Same storm. Different mindfuck.

"Figures," I muttered, deadpan, calming my pulse and the rage boiling in me. "You gonna let her tear you apart again?"

His jaw tightened till I thought it might crack. "You know I can't do that," he growled.

"Then start fucking acting like it," I snapped back. "Lucky for your sorry ass, I'm here to keep you from losing your mind when it comes to her. Just like I did at Colt's wedding. You're welcome, by the way."

And that's when he cracked.

He didn't say a word—just sagged forward, and I caught him. Not soft, not gentle. I don't do gentle. Just solid enough to hold him up while his storm burned itself out.

He trembled against me, shaking, breaths coming out in sharp, broken bursts. Blood on his knuckles, sweat dripping down his face.

"Don't... don't leave me alone, Lena," he rasped, voice shredded, like the words had to claw their way out of him.

"I'm not going anywhere," I told him, steady as bedrock. "Not tonight. Not with you like this."

I thumbed out a text.

Won't be home. It's Ash. Yeah, you already know. A heads-up next time would've been nice.

Then all hell broke loose again.

He tore into the shop—wrenches flying, cans rolling, a bike tipping over with a squeal of rubber. I dodged debris, cursing under my breath. "Goddamn you, Sloane," I hissed.

Hours crawled by.

I just stood there—arms crossed, jaw tight—watching the man I'd spent five years piecing back together come undone like it was all for fucking nothing. Every late night, every bandaged fist, every lecture about not letting a ghost own him... gone. Evaporated the second her name hit the air.

I remembered nights on the floor beside him, whispering into the dark to keep him steady while he cried for her. The helplessness when he pushed too far, when he shattered too loud. And now, here it all was again—raw, jagged, bleeding.

My chest ached for him. My heart completely shattered.
For the boy I met at twelve who'd become my anchor, my best friend, my biggest pain in the ass in life.

I disliked Sloane with every ounce of my being. I'd say I hated her but I don't hate anybody. But she's just that damn close to making me. She'd be the first.

I use to like her, thats the crazy part. Until I seen what she'd do to Ash every single time. He only ever comes undone when it comes to her. The man I know that never breaks for any motherfucker will be down on his knees, bawling, begging me to take his pain away when it comes to her. And God, I wished with everything in me that I could.

Eventually, exhaustion took him down.
He slumped to the floor, trembling, fists still twitching like he couldn't stop fighting even 8n his sleep. I sat beside him, pressed my shoulder against his back, wrapped an arm around him to keep him grounded in something solid.

By dawn, I was waking up, sore as hell and covered in grease and regret from sleeping on the floor. My body ached, it was so tense from Ash's spiral that I hadn't relaxed the whole damn night. My arm was still draped around him as if holding him alone could take his pain away.

The shop looked like a war zone—dented walls, splintered wood, blood on concrete, everywhere. Tools, debris, and bike parts from one end of it to the other. The punching bag lay shredded on the floor in the corner. Again.

I moved my arm and Ash stirred, eyes shot open. The storm wasn't gone—just waiting. Coiled. Quiet. Lethal. Ready to strike.

He rolled over, jumped up, and grabbed his jacket, boots

scraping. I caught his shoulder, fingers pressing just hard enough to remind him I was still there.

"Where the hell are you going?" I asked, voice low, tired.

"Quinn's," he said. "She'll be there. Sloane's there. I... I need to see her."

I wanted to stop him. God, I did. I wanted to save him from her, from himself. But I knew it wouldn't do a damn bit of good to try. When it came to her, he had to find out for himself, he made that clear to me before. So I just nodded and dropped my hand in defeat.

He didn't look back. Not at me. Not at the wreckage he'd made of his shop. He just walked out, fire burning in his chest like it had never gone out. He was on a mission and he was bound to see it through.

His Harley roared to life, echoing through the morning fog. I stood there, grease-stained and bone-tired, body and heart aching, watching him vanish down the road toward the one woman who'd always been his undoing.

This shitshow wasn't over.
Not by a long shot. Not even close.

Hell—this was just the prelude.

Chapter 24

The knock at Quinn's door was more like a warning shot. Heavy. Demanding.

I froze in the kitchen, coffee cup trembling in my hand. Quinn glanced at me, wide-eyed, then back at the door.

"Oh shit," she breathed, realization hitting us both at once.

My stomach plummeted. I already knew. I knew that knock anywhere.

When Quinn opened the door, there he was—Ash Walker. Leather jacket. Jaw tight. Cocky smirk cutting through the storm in his eyes.

"Well, well." His voice dripped with mockery. "Look who decided to crawl back into town. I knew you couldn't stay away from me."

My throat tightened, but I forced my chin up. "What the hell are you doing here, Ash?"

"What am I doing here?" He laughed—humorless—stepping past Quinn like the place belonged to him. The heat of him hit first—like the air itself was charged with danger.

"You disappear for five fucking years. Ghost me like I never meant a motherfuckin' thing to you. Then you come back, stir up all this bullshit I've buried so deep, and think I'm just gonna stay away?"

I scoffed, though my throat burned. "You should've stayed away. That's what you're good at, right?"

The muscle in his jaw flexed. He stepped closer. Too close. Close enough that I could smell leather and cologne—the scent that had once been home and ruin all at once.

Quinn raised her hands. "Okay, I think I'm gonna go..." She edged backward toward the hall.

"Stay," Ash snapped, eyes never leaving mine. "You might wanna see how your girl here rips people apart for sport."

My cheeks flamed. "You don't get to storm in here and—"

"Oh, I get to do whatever the fuck I want." He stalked closer, the air between us crackling like a live wire. "You think you can run away, forget me, forget us, and I'm gonna let you live your life in peace? In your fuckin' dreams, princess."

My voice wavered, though I fought to keep it steady. "I didn't come back here for you."

"Bullshit." He crowded me, heat rolling off him, his smirk a dangerous slash. "Just like I told you at Colt's wedding—I'll always be in the back of your mind. You're mine and you know it. You came back wanting me to find you. And guess what, baby? Here I am." He smiled and those dimples made my knees weak.

My pulse thundered in my throat. His nearness was intoxicating and infuriating all at once. I could feel the brush of his jacket against my arm, the weight of him pressing closer.

"If you came here to fight—"

His smirk deepened, dimples cutting sharp. "I didn't come here to fight. But if that's what you want, I'll give it to you." He winked, and I forgot how to breathe.

For a second, neither of us moved. Just heavy breaths. The ache of five years bled into the air like gasoline begging for a match.

God, I hated myself for how much my body still remembered him. How badly it wanted to close the inches between us. I wanted to push him away—and pull him in all at once.

Ash leaned in, close enough for me to feel the rough scrape of his breath against my cheek. His hand brushed my wrist, light, teasing, like a claim. His voice dropped, dark, cruel, intoxicating.

"Tell me, Sloane... after all these years, do you still fall apart the second I say your name?"

The way he said it wasn't a question. It was a knife. A dare. A memory clawing its way out of the dark and dragging me right back under.

My body betrayed me—heat flooding low, breath shattering. Every nerve on fire, every thought screaming at me to run. And from the smirk on his mouth, he knew it. Knew just how much power he still held over me.

By now, Quinn had excused herself, muttering something about not wanting front-row seats to the apocalypse—and in the same breath warning us not to fuck on her couch. We barely heard her.

Ash's eyes lingered on me, sharp and merciless, like he could read every secret I'd buried.

"I'll always have that hold on you, Sloane. Just know that."

I swallowed hard. "No—" I started.

"You think you can just come back and not deal with the wreck of me you fucking created, Sloane? You think it works that way?" He interrupted, his voice was low, dangerous. "I bared everything to you—everything—for you to walk out on me like we haven't spent the last two decades bleeding each other dry just to see who survives."

The words gutted me. *Two decades* of the inevitable pull we had. Every fight, every kiss, every lie, every night tangled in sheets and shadows—I felt them all like ghosts on my skin.

And lord, I still wanted him. The craving was poison, but I wanted the hit anyway. Even though I knew there was no antidote.

"I didn't come back for you! I came back for my life!" I snapped, my voice cracking under the weight of it.

He laughed, humorless, closing the space between us until he towered over me, eyes locked on mine with such violent emotion it nearly knocked the air from my chest.

"Your life?" His tone dripped venom. "Or just the part of it that's too scared to admit it misses me?"

Cocky bastard.

Ash reached up and slid a strand of my hair behind my ear, almost daring me to stop him.

The breath hitched in my throat before I could stop it. A sharp, unguarded gasp. His smirk told me he noticed. Of course he fucking noticed.

"You're impossible," I spat, shaking my head, trying to sound strong even as my hands trembled and my knees threatened to give out.

"Impossible?" His grin widened, dimples cutting sharp. His hand cupped my neck, strong, forcing me to look up at him. He leaned in close, voice a low burn in my ear.

"No, Sloane... I'm inevitable."

He pulled back just an inch, smile widening, eyes blazing into mine like he'd branded me with the truth.

And then—just like that—he turned and walked away.

Left me reeling. His words slicing deeper than any touch ever could.

I stood frozen, heart slamming against my ribs, eyes wide in shock that we'd just been face-to-face after five years of trying to forget, staring straight into each other's souls. Lips almost touching. Breath almost shared.

And then... that damn word again.

And the sound of his Harley rumbling as it sped away.

Dangerous. Reckless. Tortured.

Ash Walker.

Chapter 25

The sound of Ash's Harley faded, but the echo didn't. It was torture. My pulse still raced, my hands trembling, my chest tight with fire. I was supposed to be fine, perfectly composed—but every inch of me betrayed me. Every breath, every brush of air against my skin dragged me back to him.

I remembered the slam of that door, the click echoing through the silence, Ash's gaze dark with hunger. I knew I was in trouble. In one smooth motion, he tugged my panties aside and bent me over the cool porcelain sink.

"Oh, fuck," I gasped, my body folding under the weight of want and everything he always made me feel.

"You like that?" he growled against my ear, his voice thick with lust, his breath hot and dangerous. Before I could respond, he buried himself deep inside me, stealing the air from my lungs.

My back arched, my hands clawed at the edges of the sink, and my knees nearly buckled from the sheer force of him. My body trembled, overwhelmed by the intensity, moans spilling from me like a secret I couldn't hold back. The porcelain was cold under my palms, but it was his heat and his unrelenting rhythm, that seared me to the bone.

I hated how easily I opened for him. Hated how the ache between my legs wasn't nearly as sharp as the ache he always left in my chest.

Each thrust tore through me, pleasure and pain tangled together until I couldn't tell where one ended and the other began.

He could feel me tightening around him, my body betraying me, dragging him deeper, harder, like my need was a chain binding us both. With every broken moan, it felt like he needed me more; with every shuddering thrust, my soul reached for his—aching not just for his body, but for everything he was. Everything I couldn't stand, and everything I couldn't live without.

His hand tangled in my hair, yanking me back until his mouth was on my neck, his teeth scraping skin like he wanted to mark me, claim me. And I wanted it. God help me, I wanted it—wanted him—so damn bad.

I could tell he hated it—how good I felt, how familiar I was every time. How I still fit him like a fucking glove. And I knew—he fucking knew—he'd leave me aching. Not just in my body, but in that deeper, crueler place he always manages to touch no matter how much damage he'd done.

"Goddamn it, Sloane," he groaned, his voice breaking against my ear, half-growl, half-confession.

And then he thrust so deep, so complete, I shattered. My release ripped through me, violent and unrelenting, pulling his out of him like a trigger neither of us could stop. My body clamped around him, wrecked by him, ruined by him—again.

When it was over, my knees shook so bad I could barely hold myself up, chest heaving, heart pounding like it wanted to tear itself out.

I didn't say a word—couldn't—as he slipped out and tugged his shirt back on like nothing happened.

When I finally dared to look, he had that grin. That goddamn cocky grin. The one that said he knew exactly what the hell he'd just done to me. And I knew I'd never be free of it. Of him.

And just like that, he turned and was gone.

And it was then that I realized I was still bent over that damn sink.

Quinn's voice yanked me out of the memory before I drowned completely, her worried face blurred somewhere in front of me.

I was here, not there. Safe—for now. But the fire Ash left in me wasn't safe. It clawed at my chest, burning, begging, promising it would follow me no matter how far I ran.

The apartment pressed in on me like a coffin. Too tight. Too small. I bolted—keys fumbling in my hands, lungs desperate for air as I damn near ran to the car.

The engine roared like my own spiral as I sped through streets that hadn't changed, past the morning fog curling low around lampposts, trying to outrun a ghost I could never outrun.

I was pissed at myself for throwing away the only safety I've ever felt, the only calm that ever kept me sane. I walked away from the man that made the most sense. Because the heart wants what the heart wants. Even if it knows it'll get crushed in the process.

I drove around the old town I knew so well in circles trying to wrap my head around the reckless choices I've made in my life

Until I came to a resting place.

Until my tires crunched over gravel I knew too well.

Our spot. The football field.

One of the places that had held every stolen second, every kiss, every touch that broke me open.

Why here? Why the hell would I do this to myself?

The bleachers dug into my palms as I sat, trembling, wishing I could scrub him from my skin. But all I could feel was the crack in his voice, the hunger in his eyes, the ache I'd left behind in him.

And the guilt— oh God, that fuckin' guilt— it devoured me alive.

Because I hadn't just left Ash. I'd wrecked him. I'd taken every desperate touch, and gasp and claim, every confession when he'd spilled his heart to me, and I'd consumed that man whole—then walked the fuck out, like I didn't just shatter both of us like broken glass, leaving shards of us scattered, with nothing but fragments of a love that was too fractured to ever be whole again.

And God, the way that man had looked at me. Pain. Confusion. Need. Anger. So much. There was so damn much in his eyes. The way they had branded into me like fire. I hated myself for it. Hated that part of me still craved him. Hated that I remembered the way he had taken me apart and put me back together, only to rip me wide open all over again, even now—in the quiet of early morning, in the ache in my chest, in the throbbing still lingering between my legs.

Every memory of us felt like a trap. That reckless, all-consuming love that had always ended in heartbreak and wreckage—it was the only thing that ever made me feel alive, and the only thing that ever left me devastated and torn apart too.

And now I knew: giving in again wouldn't just destroy me. It would destroy him too.

But some things are inevitable...

The gravel crunched behind me, low and deliberate, and my whole body went rigid.

No Harley this time. Just the slow drag of boots across the earth.

I didn't have to look. My pulse already told me who it was.

Chapter 26

"Funny." His voice carried over me like smoke, rough and sharp. "You always did run here when you couldn't handle me."

My chest tightened, and I kept my eyes fixed on the field, like maybe if I ignored him, he'd vanish. But of course he didn't. He never did.

"Go home, Ash." My voice cracked, weak armor against the storm.

He came closer, his presence so strong I swore the air bent around him. "Can't. Not when you're here. Not when you look like this."

I snapped my head toward him, fire in my veins. "Like what? Like a fucking disaster? Congratulations, Ash—you made me this way."

"A goddamn sexy one." That grin. That stupid grin. And then it vanished, replaced by torment carved deep in his eyes.

"Don't act like you're the only one bleeding here, Sloane. You think you walking away didn't gut me? You don't even fucking know! You left me while I slept, in the middle of the goddamn night, after I FINALLY told you I fuckin' loved you! Ghosted me, skipped state, changed your number, swore Colt and Quinn to secrecy. You have no fuckin' clue what that did to me. Nor did you even care considering you were going to marry someone that wasn't me!!!" His voice cracked.

I felt his pain; betrayal and hurt cutting through his gaze as his eyes started glassing over, clearly holding back tears.

His words were knives, slicing deep, dragging open wounds I'd tried to stitch shut years ago, cutting new ones I didn't realize I'd made myself.

I shook my head hard, tears stinging my eyes.

"How do you know I'm not still gonna marry him?" I spat, pissed that he thought he knew everything.

"You wouldn't be here if you were." His voice low, was so matter-of-fact it made me roll my eyes, as the tears I'd been holding back dropped a little. I instantly wiped them away.

Silence pressed between us.

"You don't get to play victim. You ruined me plenty." I said breaking the silence.

He stepped closer, close enough his heat rolled over me, close enough I could feel the ghost of his hand at my waist even though he hadn't even touched me.

"And you ruined me right back... Although I'd say you dug the knife a little fucking deeper. Don't pretend you didn't. And don't pretend you don't feel this. Right here."

He brushed his knuckles up the inside of my arm, feather-light, gone before I could even flinch. But the burn stayed—wildfire in my veins.

"Stop," I whispered, breath shaky.

"Stop what? Breathing you in? Remembering every sound you make when you fall apart for me?" His voice was low, hungry, dangerous. "You still ache for me, Sloane. I can see it."

I shoved at his chest, weak, furious. "You don't know what the fuck I feel."

He caught my wrist—not hard, just firm, impossible to ignore. Our eyes locked, rage and hurt sparking like electricity.

"I know you're lying." His jaw ticked, voice raw with pain. "Because I'm still yours. Every fucked-up piece of me. That's why you're here. That's why you won't marry him. And you hate me for it."

"I do," I whispered, but it came out broken. My throat burned with the lie.

His forehead dipped close—too close—our breaths tangling. "Then prove it. Tell me you don't want me."

My lips parted, trembling. I couldn't. God, I couldn't. The truth was a live wire between us, humming, dangerous, ready to burn us both down.

I almost kissed him. Or he almost kissed me. Either way, one more second and we would've been gone with the autumn wind.

But he stopped.

He fucking stopped.

The smirk was gone. What replaced it was worse—raw, furious ache carved into every line of his face. "That's what I thought." His voice broke at the edges.

I tore my wrist free, stumbling back like I'd been burned alive. "You're poison," I spat, voice shaking, "and I'm done fuckin' drinking it."

But my body betrayed me, swaying toward him, craving that poison like air.

His eyes burned darker than lust. "You'll come back. You always come back. You can't quit me, Sloane. I'm in your veins."

I hated that he was right.

His words hung heavy, true, *poisonous.*

You can't quit me. I'm in your veins.

I should've walked away. Should've put distance between us before I drowned in him all over again. But my feet wouldn't move. My whole body leaned toward him instead, traitorous, greedy for one more hit of his fire.

Ash must've seen it. His jaw flexed, his hand twitched like he wanted to reach for me but didn't. His restraint was it's own torment—because the space between us was agony, and he knew it.

"You think this is a choice?" His voice was ragged, stripped bare. "It's not. You and me? We're already ruined. Already branded. You don't get to erase us, Sloane. You can't."

My chest heaved, a sob clawing up my throat I barely swallowed down. "And what do you want from me, huh? To admit I still want you? That I still dream about you, still wake up aching for you like a goddamn fool after all these years?"

His eyes locked on mine, blazing. "Yes."

The word was a brand, searing me where I stood. My lips parted, trembling, but no sound came out. I couldn't admit it. I couldn't give him that victory, that satisfaction. But I couldn't deny it either—my body had already given me away when it leaned toward him, practically begging him to take me right there.

The silence stretched taut and dangerous, like lightning seconds before it splits the sky.

And then he stepped back.

The distance hit like a gunshot. My body lunged before I caught myself, nails digging into my palms.

"Fuck you," I choked, hating the tremor in my voice.

His eyes swept over me one last time, slow and claiming, memorizing every broken piece of me. "Already did," he murmured, dark and final.

Bastard.

Then he turned, boots crunching gravel, leaving me with the ghost of his heat, his touch, his almost-kiss still searing my skin.

Destroyed.
Ruined.
Wrecked.
Again.

Only this time, the silence didn't feel empty.
It felt like a curse.
Like his hands were wrapped around my throat as he walked away.
Like he took my ability to breathe with him.

And I knew—no matter how far I ran, no matter how many times I swore I was done—
Ash Walker would always be the one thing I couldn't escape.

Because the truth was brutal, undeniable, clawing at my chest:
I wasn't scared of us wrecking each other again.

I was scared of what would happen when we finally didn't.

Chapter 27

The steering wheel was slick beneath my palms. My chest still felt like his fingerprints were pressed into it—bruised, branded—and I hated myself for how part of me already missed him.

I needed to get it together. To breathe. To pretend like I didn't give a shit.

But of course, the universe had the cruelest sense of humor—because the only place I could think to go was Colt's. My brother. My anchor. My twin who had no idea how twisted I still was inside.

I pulled into his driveway, heart pounding for a whole different reason now. Ash Walker's ghost still clung to me, and now I had to face the one person who would hate it most if he ever knew.

And then there was her. Colt's wife, Elise. Sweet, steady, perfect...completely put together and not ready for the storm about to walk into her house.

I didn't knock. I shoved the door open and stumbled inside—hands trembling, stomach twisting, chest on fire.

Fuck. Fuck. Fuck.

Colt was there before I could blink, filling the doorway like a wall I couldn't move through.

Broad-shouldered, solid from years of football and fighting and training at *Underground*, with dark blond hair with a reddish tint to it, always a little messy and green eyes sharp enough to slice through every lie I'd ever tried to tell him. He carried a calm you didn't question—steady, grounded, unshakable. My opposite in every way. Except looks. I pretty well mirrored him.

And he already knew.

"Sloane...I was hoping you would visit soon." he asked, pulling me into a hug that felt more like a searchlight.

"Sorry, had to recover." My voice cracked.

"Shit." The word left him sharp and low, like a curse he couldn't hold back. His eyes narrowed, pinning me. "You've seen him."

I froze. "...Yep. Of course I have." My head dropped.

"I know. I can tell." Colt's voice was even, but his jaw was tight. "You're coming undone as we speak."

He wasn't wrong.

From the kitchen, Elise appeared—big brown eyes soft, dark wavy hair pulled back loose, her smile the kind that made anyone feel safe. "Oh, honey. I've got you a drink." She pressed a whiskey on ice into my hand. I threw it back without hesitation. "Thanks. I needed that." as she disappeared back into the kitchen with quiet grace.

Then I looked at Colt, the weight in my chest pressing harder. "I can't stop looking for him in everyone I see. I broke it off with Cage-for exactly that reason." My voice shook, small. His eyes widened.

"He still fucking haunts me, Colt. And I want him more than anything. I don't even care if it destroys me this time." Tears pricked, hot and merciless. There was no point in lying to my twin. He always saw through me anyways.

Colt's jaw flexed, calm fire burning under those blue green eyes. "Sloane, you two are poisonous together. I'll never understand why you can't stop tearing each other apart."

My mind flashed back to the last time he'd said almost the same thing—

"Look, even though I don't like it, it's not something y'all have to hide anymore. Neither of you were very good at it anyway. I knew from the moment I introduced you two that there was chemistry—don't insult

me by pretending I didn't. I saw the way you looked at each other. I'm your twin. You think I couldn't tell? And if I didn't give my blessing then, it'd wreck you both worse than it already had. But make no mistake—what you two have is nothing but wreckage and heartbreak. I've watched both of you come undone over the other. You think I like watching my sister and my best friend rip each other to pieces?"

Back then, I couldn't argue. Now, I still couldn't.

"Sloane, you know how this ends," Colt said, teeth clenched. "The same way it does every. Single. Time. But I won't stand in yall's way because I wish you could both stop being stubborn asses already."

When it came to Ash and me, Colt treaded carefully, like stepping barefoot through glass. He hated what we did to each other. Hated how it gutted us both.

"I know." My throat burned. "I don't know how to stop the shit we do to each other."

Colt grabbed my hand, his laugh low and sad, almost breaking. "I know. And neither can he." He sighed, shoulders sinking with the weight of it. "Just...be prepared."

I nodded, shivering from more than cold. The whiskey burned, but the memories burned more. And Ash...Ash burned almost as much as my brother's warning.

The truth—my truth—was raw and screaming beneath my ribs. Ash. Still inside me. Still haunting me. Still waiting.

I swallowed hard, forcing myself to breathe, knowing it wouldn't last.

I did this to myself. I knew what coming back here would mean. I was burning for everything I shouldn't want—for what always was and what always would be.

Even my brother knew what was coming. And you'd think that would be warning enough. That this time, I'd finally listen. That I'd listen to him, the one person who had never left me.

But I never listened. Not when it came to Ash Walker.

Chapter 28

I was already buzzing from the couple shots Elise had poured me, so I wandered downtown to the bar, looking for anything–anyone–to drag my mind away from Ash.

The streets were alive in that chaotic, Friday-night way, neon signs flickering above groups of strangers spilling onto the sidewalk, laughter mixing with the low thrum of bass from different bars bleeding into one another. My body moved through it automatically, like maybe if I stayed in motion, my thoughts wouldn't catch up.

Inside the bar, the music hit like a pulse, heavy and relentless, vibrating in my chest. I ordered a whiskey on the rocks, the clink of ice loud in my ears, and slipped outside to the patio.

Leaning against the railing, I let the night air wash over me, cooler than the thick warmth of the crowd inside. My fingers itched, restless, so I pulled out the Backwoods I'd rolled earlier at Colt's. We'd smoked one together before I left, and it had been the only time that day I'd felt remotely calm. Now I needed that calm again, something to do with my hands, something to focus on besides the reel of memories I didn't want.

I sparked it, inhaled, and let the smoke curl out in a slow exhale. My chest loosened. Not much, but enough.

Then *she* appeared.

Blonde bob cut, sharp and glossy under the patio lights. Piercing blue eyes that found me instantly, like I'd been waiting for her without knowing it. A silver nose ring glinted when she tilted her head, and when she licked her lips, I caught the flash of a tongue piercing catching the glow from the bar's sign. Her cropped leopard-print belly shirt clung to her frame like it had been designed to showcase her confidence, and a serpent tattoo coiled up her right leg, sharp and sinuous–the kind of detail that demanded attention. Everything about her screamed confident. Playful. Dangerous. Magnetic.

My chest tightened instantly. She wasn't Ash—thank God—but she was exactly what I needed to forget him for a while. I'd never been with a woman before, but I wasn't opposed. Anybody was a better idea than Ash.

She slid into the seat beside me, drink in hand, close enough that her warmth brushed mine.

"Mind if I join you?" Her voice was low, teasing—provocative. A dare.

"Not at all," I said, trying to sound casual, though my pulse had other ideas.

We started with small talk—the music, the DJ, joking about how questionable the playlist was—but everything about her pulled me in. The bob of her hair. The glint of her piercing blue eyes. The playful curve of her lips. The serpent tattoo winding up her leg as she shifted in the seat. Every glance, every smirk felt like it had been made to reel me closer.

Her leg brushed mine under the table, feather-light, teasing. Heat coiled low in my stomach. Her fingers flicked against mine when she reached for her drink, deliberate, playful, lingering just long enough to spark. I noticed the way another tattoo peeked beneath her shirt when she leaned back, the slope of her waist, the mischievous sparkle in her eyes. She was teasing me—and I liked it.

She nodded toward the Backwoods in my hand. "You gonna share that, or are you planning to keep it all to yourself?"

Her grin was lazy, confident, daring me. Without thinking, I passed it over. She leaned in, lips brushing the tip as she pulled in a slow drag, eyes never leaving mine. Smoke curled from her mouth in a silver ribbon, hanging between us like something intimate, something claimed.

"Smooth," she said, handing it back. Her fingers lingered against mine. "Rolled nice, too."

I shrugged, pretending it wasn't the compliment that got me, but the way her lips had pressed to where mine just were.

We passed it back and forth, shoulders close, laughter coming easier with every inhale. The smoke softened the edges of everything—the noise of the city, the burn of my whiskey, the memories clawing at me from the inside. For a few minutes, it was just her and me, sharing the same breath, caught in the same haze.

"You don't seem like the type who hangs out here much," she said, exhaling smoke through her nose, eyes glinting.

"Guess I needed a change of scenery."

"Or maybe you needed company," she countered, lips curving in a smirk that was all challenge.

Her words landed sharper than I expected, but instead of pulling back, I found myself leaning in. Our conversation slipped into something more personal—laughing about work, swapping silly habits, little confessions.

Beneath every word was a hum of tension. My focus narrowed to the way she tipped her head back when she laughed, the flash of silver on her tongue, the way her leg pressed against mine and didn't move away.

Before I knew it, I was confessing I'd never been with a woman before.

Her smirk widened. "Don't worry, babe—this ain't my first rodeo." She winked, and something electric shot straight through me.

"Want to get out of here?" she asked suddenly, voice low and daring, eyes glittering like a challenge.

Without thinking, I nodded.

The walk to her apartment was electric, alive with endless possibility. The streets buzzed with neon, groups stumbling from bar to bar, laughter echoing off the buildings. Every brush of shoulders, every playful glance, every shared laugh and subtle touch sent sparks through me. She'd bump into me intentionally, shoulder grazing mine, then flash me that mischievous grin. Her hand trailed against my arm when she leaned in to point out some mural on the wall, like she needed an excuse to touch me again.

The air smelled like fried food from a food truck parked on the corner, like cigarettes, like the faint crispness of fall trying to muscle it's way in. And under all of it was her—vanilla and smoke, sharp and sweet, enough to make my head light.

For the first time in a long time, I wasn't thinking about Ash. Not about California. Not about the wreckage I'd left behind in both places. Just the curve of her waist, the serpent tattoo coiling up her leg, the way her cropped belly shirt revealed a sliver of stomach with more ink and a belly button ring when she moved.

By the time we reached her building, she had all of me—my focus, my pulse, my attention. She fumbled for her keys, and I watched the sway of her hips, the tilt of her smile when she caught me staring again.

We stepped inside, the door clicking shut behind us, muffling the noise of the city. Suddenly it was just me and her, and the crisp autumn breeze that had followed us inside like a secret. She pressed a hand to my chest, guiding me backward into her apartment, and I let her.

She wasn't just a distraction. She was a spark—immediate, playful, sexual, irresistible.

And I didn't care where it led. All I knew was that, for tonight, it wasn't Ash consuming me. It was her.

Chapter 29

Her apartment smelled faintly of vanilla and smoke, just like her, warm and unfamiliar, like a memory I didn't realize I wanted. The scent clung to the air, wrapping around me as if it belonged to the walls themselves, soaked into the fabric of the couch, hidden in the grain of the wood floors. It wasn't homey, exactly—more sharp than soft—but it pulled me in. Comforting in a way I didn't expect, intoxicating in a way I didn't want to question.

The second the door clicked shut behind us, she grabbed me by the front of my shirt and tugged me close, lips crashing against mine with a force that stole my breath. There was no hesitation, no careful testing of limits. It was want, plain and unfiltered, and it burned through me before I could catch my balance.

Her tongue brushed mine, teasing and insistent, while her hands slid up my sides, fingers trailing under my shirt with a confidence that sent sparks racing across my skin. Her body pressed flush against me, hot and urgent, every curve fitting against mine like she'd been designed to. Every movement carried a reckless hunger I hadn't felt since Ash. It was dizzying, and I let myself drown in it.

My hands roamed without thinking, memorizing the contours of her waist, the curve of her hips, the rise and fall of her chest as she breathed against me. Her cropped shirt lifted under my fingertips, smooth skin beneath, and I gripped her tighter, greedy for the feeling. She only encouraged it, pushing herself closer, arching into me with every heartbeat.

Ash didn't exist here. Not his voice, not the pull in his eyes, not the ache he always left behind. In this apartment, there was only her—electric and daring, impossible and untouchable. Every brush of her lips, every teasing laugh that spilled against mine, made it easier to forget him, easier to slip into a fantasy where I could be someone else.

Her laughter was intoxicating, low and playful, vibrating against my mouth between kisses. It wasn't self-conscious. It wasn't hesitant. It was confident, like she already knew exactly what she was doing to me. My hands clutched her waist, pulling her impossibly closer, desperate to erase the empty space between us. She leaned in, nails grazing the back of my neck, and I shivered violently, caught somewhere between pleasure and disbelief.

When her mouth trailed down my throat, I closed my eyes and let the sensation consume me. The scrape of her teeth, the heat of her breath, the delicate sting of her piercing brushing my skin—it all blurred into something sharp and sweet. I tilted my head back, surrendering, letting myself imagine a life where I wanted someone else. Where my nights didn't revolve around memories of Ash.

Her hands tugged at the hem of my shirt, dragging it higher, and I raised my arms without hesitation. The fabric hit the floor somewhere behind me, forgotten. Her palms slid across my bare skin, warm and sure, mapping me like I was something worth knowing. My chest heaved as her lips followed, tasting, teasing, pulling a sound from me I didn't recognize as my own.

Every fleeting brush, every whispered gasp, became a small rebellion—a stolen moment that was mine alone. She was a rebellion in herself, a challenge, a dare I couldn't resist.

Her pulse raced beneath my fingertips when I touched her, fingers slipping under the waistband of her shorts. The sharp intake of her breath, the way she leaned into my touch—it sent something crashing through me. For the first time in years, I let myself breathe, fully and freely, untethered from the weight of Ash.

Her serpent tattoo caught the light when she shifted, winding across her thigh like it was alive, and I traced it with my hand, following the ink as if it could guide me somewhere new. Her eyes fluttered shut, lips parting in a sound that made heat coil low in my stomach.

This wasn't love. It wasn't forever. It wasn't even meant to be remembered in the morning. It was escape. Distraction. A single night where I could lose myself without consequences.

And yet, as her body pressed me back against the couch, as she straddled my lap and kissed me like she'd been waiting all night for this, I almost believed it could be more. Almost believed that if I held on tight enough, if I kissed her hard enough, Ash would dissolve from me completely.

Her hair brushed my face, soft and clean, smelling faintly of citrus under the smoke. Her laughter came again, softer now, more breath than sound, as if she couldn't help but enjoy the way I melted under her. She pulled back just enough to meet my eyes, her blue gaze glittering in the dim apartment light.

"You taste good," she murmured, voice husky, deliberate.

I swallowed, breath ragged. "So do you."

Her grin spread, wicked and pleased, before she leaned in again, kissing me harder. My hands slid up her back, memorizing the lines of her shoulder blades, the dip of her spine. She ground against me, slow and intentional, and I lost the thread of thought completely.

Ash wasn't here. He couldn't be. Not when she had me like this. Not when every nerve ending in my body answered to her touch.

Her shorts joined my shirt on the floor, followed by the scrape of denim, the sound of zippers, the soft rustle of fabric giving way to skin. Every new inch of her revealed left me hungrier, more desperate, like I'd been starved for this exact moment without even knowing it. She kissed me through it, steady and unrelenting, swallowing every broken sound I made as if she wanted to claim them all.

Time blurred. Minutes, hours—it didn't matter. The apartment was small, but it became a world in itself, the two of us moving through it with reckless urgency. Every wall, every surface, every kiss felt like proof that I could forget. That I could give myself away without him hovering over me.

And in the press of her body, the heat of her lips, the laughter that danced over my skin, I almost believed it could last. Almost believed I could forget.

Almost.

Chapter 30

The blinds bled pale morning light across the apartment, cutting thin shadows through the haze of smoke and candle. The scent of vanilla lingered in the sheets, mixing with sweat, making the air feel heavier than it was.

My body still hummed, loose and raw, like I'd been unraveled and left open to the world.

Her hand sifted lazily through my hair, her nails tracing my scalp in absent rhythm. Her lips were swollen, her blonde bob tangled, but she carried it like armor, even in the softness of morning.

For a moment, I let myself drift in it—the rare quiet, the strange comfort. Then her voice broke through. "So," she murmured, tone deceptively casual, "where you from originally?"

I traced the serpent inked along her thigh, my fingertip following the curve of its body. "Here but moved to Cali for a while."

Her hand stilled against me. The pause was subtle, but it made my chest tighten.

"Cali, huh?" she echoed, slow, as though tasting the word. Her gaze sharpened when it found mine, something flickering behind those bright blue eyes. "Babe..." Her voice dropped, soft but heavy. "What's your name?"

I blinked, hesitated. But the truth slipped out anyway. "Sloane...and what's yours?"

Her lips parted. Everything in her went still.

For a beat, the room was too quiet. Then came a laugh—low, shaky, disbelieving. Not the playful sound from last night, but something darker, jagged at the edges.

"Kassidy." she said her eyes dragging over me like she was cataloging every inch she'd touched, every curve she'd claimed, like she was memorizing me for evidence.

Fascination bled into something harsher—jealousy, anger—but neither won. They twisted together until I couldn't tell them apart

.

"So you're her" she whispered.
I frowned, confused. "I'm...who?"

Kassidy smiled then, but it wasn't kind. Her thumb brushed across my cheek, tender in a way that didn't match the bite in her voice.

"Now I get it," she murmured. "Why someone would burn their whole damn world down for you."
Her words hit, but I couldn't place them. My chest tightened anyway.

Before I could ask, her mouth was on mine, slower this time. Not hungry the way it had been in the dark hours before, but deliberate, weighted with things I couldn't name. She kissed me like she wanted to consume me and curse me all at once.

Her hand skimmed down my side, still bare from the night before, possessive, studying. "No wonder," she whispered against my lips, voice rough. "No fucking wonder people can't forget you."

A shiver crawled over my skin, heat sparking low, but unease threaded through it. "What are you talking about?" I asked, my voice barely more than a breath.

She didn't answer. Her nails dragged lightly down my spine, sending a violent tremor through me. Her laugh followed, sharp but quiet, like she was mocking herself more than me. "It's infuriating," she admitted, almost too soft to hear. "To finally understand."
I swallowed hard, heart hammering. "Understand what?"

Her blue eyes glittered, pinning me in place. "What it feels like to be compared to someone you've never even met."

The words struck like a match. My throat tightened, but my mind scrambled, unable to connect the pieces. Compared by who? To who? But she kissed me again before I could ask, silencing me with a heat that pulled me under.

It should've felt wrong. But it didn't. Her jealousy pressed into every kiss, her fingers gripping me tighter, as though hating me made her want me more.

She broke away, forehead pressed to mine, her breath ragged. "God, you're dangerous." The admission came out like a confession, like a curse. "And now I know why you have that hold."

The weight of her stare pressed down on me, but her hand still cupped my jaw, her thumb stroking soft, betraying the storm in her words.

I wanted to pull away, to demand clarity. But the way she looked at me—with hunger and fury knotted together—kept me frozen. My body leaned into her even as my mind screamed for answers.

Her lips found mine again, desperate, bruising, like she couldn't stop herself. Her pulse raced under my palm, proof that whatever war she was waging with herself, I was at the center of it, and she was losing.

Next thing I knew, her fingers were inside me, pressing with deliberate intent, teasing, curling, dragging me closer to the edge, over and over. Her lips grazed my ear, voice low and commanding.

"Look at me," she demanded, voice husky, low. "Arch for me, Sloane. Let go. Let me see how far I can take you."

I obeyed without thinking, body quivering, mind scattered, my breath catching in ragged gasps. Her fingers pressed with deliberate intent, teasing, curling, dragging me closer to the edge, over and over.

"Cum for me, baby," she whispered.

Shattering, my body tensed, heat coiling impossibly tight, and with a strangled cry, I came, trembling violently under her skilled, unrelenting touch. She held me through it, guiding me, claiming every shiver, every breath, until I was utterly spent, utterly hers.

I was on fire. I was lost. Confused. Caught between wanting more of her touch and wanting to run from whatever truth she was dancing around.

I didn't know then that the ghost she spoke of had a name. Didn't know that name was Ash. Didn't know that in one reckless night, I'd tied myself to his ghost again—without ever realizing it. Fucking myself in every sense of the way.

Chapter 31

The door clicked shut behind Sloane, and I exhaled slowly, realizing I'd been holding my breath. The apartment felt too quiet without her – too still, like the air hadn't caught up yet.

I leaned against the counter, the mug warm in my hands, and stared at the spot where Sloane had been just moments ago. I hadn't expected her to stay the night. Hell, I hadn't expected to like her. But Sloane had stayed – had made coffee, had laughed softly as she sat on my couch – and something about that felt dangerously intimate.

Somewhere between the second cup of coffee and a story about small-town summers, it hit me.

It's *her.*

I had almost laughed at the realization, almost spilled my drink, almost blurted it out – but I hadn't. I'd just sat there, nodding along, letting Sloane talk while inside, everything rearranged itself.

The woman I'd taken home from the bar wasn't just anyone. She was the woman Ash had never gotten over.

I set my mug down and braced my palms against the counter, staring at the smooth surface as if it might explain why my chest felt so tight.

I used to think Ash was being dramatic – clinging to the ghost of a first love because he didn't know how to move on. I used to hate him a little for it. But sitting across from Sloane this morning, I understood.

God help me, I understood.

Sloane was magnetic. Not loud or demanding, but the kind of person you couldn't look away from once you'd really seen her. There was a pull there — quiet, steady, undeniable — and I felt it in my bones.

Lord, did I feel it in my bones. That woman did something to me, awakened something in me.

The way she smiled, and those dimples shone like diamonds every time, her dermals sparkling bright. I love me a woman with piercings.

My lips curved despite myself. My pussy started throbbing.

The way her green-blue eyes would lock onto mine igniting a spark inside me I couldn't even begin to explain. The way wrapping her hair in my hand had felt as she moaned into the night, breathless, remembering how my other hand was three fingers deep inside her.

No wonder Ash couldn't let her go. And if I was honest, I didn't want to let her go either.

Images from last night rose, uninvited — Sloane's hand brushing mine, the way she tilted her head when she smiled, the sharp flash in her eyes when things had turned heated. My pulse kicked up, warmth spreading low in my pussy, causing a throbbing I couldn't ignore anymore.

I pushed away from the counter and crossed to the couch, dropping onto it with a sigh. The apartment still smelled like Sloane — perfume, coffee, a hint of shampoo — and that only made me throb harder.

I let my head fall back against the cushions, staring up at the ceiling, taking in her scent, remembering every detail of last night.

I slid my shorts to the side, sliding my finger inside my soaking wet, throbbing pussy. I felt myself instantly clench around my finger as I slid a second one in, teasing myself with each stroke, slow at first. But as I got wetter, more vivid images of Sloane — of the way she tasted, the way she felt with my fingers deep inside her aching flesh — danced in my mind. By this time, I was slamming my fingers inside my pussy so hard, so fast, as my juices erupted everywhere — all over my fingers, my clothes, the couch.

Throbbing, shaking, and aching for more, I jumped up and went to the dresser in the corner of the room, where I grabbed a rhinestone-covered vibrator out of my top drawer. Crossing the two steps to my bed, I pulled my shorts down, shoving the vibrator in with a quick motion.

I lay back and closed my eyes as my pussy awakened for another round of ecstasy, shoving the vibrator in deeper, shivering in pure delight. In and out, slow at first, going faster and deeper with every unhinged thought of Sloane – her smile, those sexy-ass dimples, those eyes that locked onto my soul. My vibrator was drenched, humming low inside me. I then used my other hand to rub my clit faster, angling my vibrator to go deeper.

Sloane's intoxicating laugh, the way she moaned for me as I licked her juices dry. Then thoughts of Ash – inside Sloane, tasting her, fucking her, loving her.

That thought sent me writhing, shattering completely around the rhinestone vibrator, breathless over the edge, pussy coiling in want and need.

Why I came so hard at the thought of them together is beyond me. But I'd never had an orgasm so intense in my life. I was a shaking, throbbing, aching, soaking, fucking wet mess.

And the thought of Sloane moaning Ash's name as he fucked the life out of her turned me on so goddamn much that I wanted to see how that went down in more than just my imagination.

I hadn't known last night who I was inviting into my bed. Hadn't known the connection I'd end up having with her. Damn sure didn't know the ties I'd have to her. But now that I did, damn, I'd do it all over again.

Because strangely, there was no anger. No jealousy. Just a strange, quiet clarity... and an attraction that felt even sharper now that I knew who Sloane was. A pull I can't walk away from.

For years, I'd resented Ash for choosing a ghost over me. But now, sitting here in the quiet aftermath of last night, I couldn't help but think maybe he hadn't been wrong to love her the way he did.

The thought made me laugh under my breath.

I still didn't know what this meant – for me, for Sloane, for Ash, for any of us.

But I knew one thing: I wanted to see Sloane again.
And it wasn't just for closure.

Chapter 32

My phone buzzed again.

Quinn.

Where the hell are you?

I didn't reply. I just grabbed my keys from my purse once I got to the bar and drove toward Quinn's.

By the time I turned onto her street, my chest was tight – because I saw a motorcycle in her driveway. My heart pounded harder as I got closer, until I realized it was Lena's motorcycle.

I forced my pulse to slow before going inside.

Quinn and Lena were curled up together on the couch, a blanket twisted around them, a movie playing low. Lena's head rested on Quinn's shoulder, Quinn's arm loose around her waist – casual, like they'd done this a hundred times before.

Quinn looked up first, her smirk lazy. "Hey. I was wondering when you'd come back."

I just stood there.

She tilted her head, like she'd been waiting for me to say something, then shrugged. "Guess it's time you know. Lena and I have been seeing each other for a while now. I haven't had a chance to tell you yet."

For a second, all I could do was blink.

"Oh," I said finally, stepping inside.

"Don't look so shocked."

“I’m not,” I muttered, even though my brain was spinning.

I should’ve left, but instead I sank into the armchair across from them.

Now that I was sitting here, I could see it.

Of course it made sense. Quinn and Lena – it was so obvious now that I thought about it.

And somehow, like everything else lately, it still traced back to him.

All ties lead back to Ash.

Because of course they fuckin' do.

The movie kept playing, but I didn’t hear a word of it. My head was too loud – full of last night with Kassidy, the way her laugh sank into my skin, the way she looked at me like she knew exactly who I was.

And Ash.

Always Ash.

The memory of him hit me hard – the way he touched me, the sound of my name in his voice. The pull between us that never really let go.

I forced myself to sit through a few more minutes of movie chatter, but I couldn’t focus. My skin felt hot, stretched too tight, like my body knew something was coming.

“Think I’m gonna crash,” I said, cutting off Quinn’s next sentence. “That spare room still good?”

“Yeah,” Quinn said, throwing me a small smile. “Fresh sheets and everything. It's yours as long as you're here, Lo. You good?”

“Yeah.” A lie. She knew.

I shut the door behind me and sat on the edge of the bed. The quiet swallowed me whole.

My phone buzzed.

I grabbed it.

Unknown number.
You done running?

I froze. There was only one person it could be. My stomach flipped.

How the hell did you get my number?

Almost instantly:

Does it matter?

My chest tightened.

Yes.

I wanted it, so I got it. You know I always get what I want.

God, I hated the way that made heat curl in my stomach.

So what do you want?

You.

I pressed my lips together so hard they hurt.

You don't get to say things like that.

Then stop making me want to.

My heart thudded so loud it drowned out the noise from the living room.

You think this is a game?

No. I think this is the part where you stop pretending you don't want me too. We both know why you came back.

I threw the phone on the bed, but the buzzing kept coming.

You can keep running. Or you can come find me.

I stared at the screen until the letters blurred.

Why do you always do this to me?

There was a long pause this time, before he replied—

Because you let me.

I sank back on the bed, heart hammering. My hands ached from clenching the phone so tight, my body wound too tight with fury and something else I didn't want to name.

I didn't answer him. Couldn't.

I just lay there staring at the ceiling, Quinn and Lena's muffled laughter carrying down the hallway – a sound from a world I couldn't seem to belong to anymore.

The phone buzzed again. My chest tightened before I even read it.

Do you remember that time I was locked up and we were on the phone, and I had you play with yourself while I listened?

I froze. My fingers clutched the blanket, heart hammering.

God.

I remembered.

"If *I was there right now... do you know what I'd do to you, Sloane?" His voice had been a growl, deep enough to vibrate through the cheap plastic receiver and straight into me.*

"No... tell me," I'd whispered, breathless.

"Get your toy out of your nightstand."

I'd hesitated. He'd known.

"Be a good girl. Do as I say."

My body had obeyed before my brain could catch up, the sound of him in my ear winding around me like barbed wire.

"Now push it in... slow, deep thrusts. Twist it clockwise... think of me inside you, over and over, until you can't hold back and you cum—hard and long—all over us both."

I'd done it, each word of his making me wetter, needier, until I'd been nothing but sound and heat and motion, coming apart on his command, moaning his name like a prayer, imagining him inside me as I squirt all over myself.

"That's right, baby. I love hearing your juices... the sound you make when you cum for me."

And then—

"Try not to make a mess of your sheets without me, Sloane... though I kind of love it when you do."

Click.

He'd hung up before the minute the automated voice told us we had left was even up, leaving me shaking, wrecked, clutching the buzzing toy like a lifeline, my body a puddle of ache and want.

Memory lane was a motherfucker, let me tell ya. I shook my head trying to shake the memory away.

Another text.

Let's make it happen again. Grab your toy for me Sloane.

Unbelievable. The nerve of him. I responded with:

No Ash Cameron I'm not doing this with you. Goodnight.

So good you say my middle name too, huh?

I could just picture that smug, cocky grin of his, and my blood started boiling. Exasperating.

I threw my phone beside me on the bed and grabbed my toy out of my bag.

I stared at it in my hand, chest heaving. My whole body felt tight, restless.

My phone buzzed again.

Don't make me wait. Be a good girl and do as I say.

"Goddamn you, Ash," I muttered – grabbing my toy pulling my panties down, the toy buzzing low in my hand.

Start slow. I want to imagine how wet you are for me.

I slid it in, slow and deep, my breath stuttering as my body clenched around it.

That's it. Twist it. I want to hear it.

I did, the sound of my wetness filling the quiet room, obscene and loud enough I almost dropped the phone.

Fuck... I swear I can hear you. Go deeper.

I thrust harder, hips rolling off the bed, chasing the high building in my gut.

Grip that toy like it's me. Ride it like you're riding my cock.

"Fuck," I gasped, obeying without thinking, pumping it faster, twisting with every stroke. My thighs were soaked, sheets already damp, my whole body hot and wild.

Don't stop. I want to hear you scream for me, Sloane.

That was all it took. My back arched, my legs trembled, and I shattered – the orgasm ripping through me so hard my vision blurred.

I moaned his name, loud and broken, my hand still gripping the toy.

But before I could breathe, the phone buzzed again.

Don't you dare stop. Go again.

My stomach flipped.

Ash–

No excuses. You're not done until I say you're done.

A shiver raked through me. My body ached, already hypersensitive, but I obeyed – sliding the toy back in and biting back a whimper as my body clenched tight around it.

That's it. Take it. Faster this time.

I obeyed, thrusting quick and deep, my breath coming in ragged gasps, every nerve ending screaming from overstimulation.

I can just imagine how damn good you feel. You like it when I wreck you, don't you?

God help me, I did.

My second orgasm hit like a freight train — harder, meaner — leaving me trembling, thighs quaking, sweat slicking my skin.

One more. Make it sloppy.

I groaned, desperate, but didn't stop. My body moved on instinct, chasing that third high until I was soaked, messy, legs spread wide and aching.

When I finally came again, it was almost painful — my body jerking, tears pricking my eyes as the orgasm dragged out long and raw.

I collapsed, the toy falling from my hand, chest heaving like I'd just run miles.

Good girl. That's how I like you — ruined and thinking of me.

Chapter 33

The sun was too bright.

I blinked against it, groaning as I rolled onto my stomach. My body felt heavy, like I'd been hit by something and left to recover in this bed that wasn't mine.

Quinn's house was silent except for the faint hum of the fridge down the hall. It should've felt comforting. Safe.

It didn't.

Because my phone was on the pillow next to me, screen dark but alive in a way that made my chest thrum.

Last night replayed in flashes: my toy, his words, the way my body had betrayed me even as my brain told me to stop. Over and over again.

God, what the hell was wrong with me?

I told myself not to check my phone. I told myself to get up, get dressed, pretend none of it happened.

But of course, I looked.

One new message. Sent at 3:04 a.m.

Bet you came thinking about me again before you fell asleep.

My stomach flipped. Anger. Lust. Everything I wasn't supposed to feel.

I should delete it.

Instead, I stared until my hands shook.

A knock at the door made me jump.

"You awake?" Quinn's voice floated through the wood.

"Yeah," I rasped.

"You want coffee? Lena's making breakfast."

Of course she was. Of course they were out there, domestic and perfect.

"I'll be out in a minute."

I dragged myself out of bed and to the bathroom, splashing cold water on my face until the mirror stopped showing someone who looked wrecked. By the time I padded into the kitchen, Quinn and Lena were leaning against the counter, plates in hand.

"Morning," Lena said, eyes sharp.

"Morning," I muttered, grabbing a piece of toast.

Quinn smiled softly. "Sleep okay?"

"Sure." Lie.

Lena's gaze lingered too long before she looked away, like she wanted to ask something but didn't.

Lena's never really liked me. She's Ash's best friend and trusted sidekick. They've been inseparable since they were kids. That history made every glance from her feel like judgment – like a lifetime of knowing him better than anyone, and knowing I wasn't supposed to hurt him, had no right to.

And then I remembered the day she confronted me after I went on a date with Ash's *Underground* rival Dante, after I'd found out about Ash's name on Ember's neck.

Her eyes cut into me, sharp and unflinching. "You think you can just... rip his fuckin' heart out and walk away?" Her voice trembled, half fury, half disgust. "You don't get to touch him like that. You don't get to break him—and you damn sure better not ever come crawling back after this."

I wanted to argue, to explain, to make her see it wasn't that simple. But I couldn't. Her words pressed down on me heavier than anything Ash had ever said. The truth I'd been running from hit me like a stone: I had hurt him. I had hurt him over and over again. And this last time I had crossed a line I could never take back.

Lena didn't hate me. Not exactly. Or at least I didn't think so. But she didn't trust me either. And that scared me more than anything – because if Lena didn't believe I could be trusted with Ash, how could I ever forgive myself for what I did to him?

Later, when Quinn handed me a spare key and told me to make myself at home, I mumbled a thanks and escaped back to the guest room. Door closed. Lock clicked. I sat on the edge of the bed, phone in my lap like a live wire.

You're exasperating!

His reply was instant.

But yet here you are... still talking to me.

I clenched the phone.

You have no right to—

I have every right. You're mine, Sloane. You always have been.

My chest thudded. I hated him. And I wanted him so badly it hurt.

I stared at the ceiling until the silence was unbearable. Finally, I typed:

You don't get to call me that anymore.

Then stop being mine.

That's not how this works, Ash.

That's exactly how it works. You've been running for years. But you came back for me... still answering me... still thinking about me when you touch yourself.

Heat flushed my face.

You're disgusting.

Maybe. But you loved that shit last night.

I threw the phone down like it burned, pacing. God, he was infuriating. And worse, he was right.

The phone buzzed again. I shouldn't have even looked.

You can't keep doing this halfway shit. Either you block me or you come see me.

You don't get to give me ultimatums.

I *just did. Decide, Sloane. I'm not playing this game anymore.*

I sank onto the edge of the bed, heart hammering. He wasn't going to let me hide. He never does.

And if I say no?

You can't avoid the inevitable forever, Sloane. How long do you think you can run?

That damn word again. *Inevitable.*

The air felt too thick to breathe. I squeezed the phone, vision blurring. Somewhere down the hall, Quinn laughed at something Lena said. Warm. Easy. Normal. Uncomplicated.

I wished any part of this was uncomplicated.

Chapter 34

I rolled a Backwoods using the nightstand next to the bed and walked to the kitchen, grabbing a bottle of water from the fridge. I grabbed my hoodie from the front door closet, stepping outside to smoke. I was breathing in the smoke, letting it calm my nerves, letting it blur my thoughts for just a second, taking in the nice autumn air.

Then I felt it – eyes on me. I froze. My chest hitched.

The screen door creaked, and out stepped Lena.

I knew this was coming eventually.

Her gaze was ice, sharp enough to slice through the smoke curling around me. She didn't waste time.

"Look, Sloane. We need to talk."

I opened my mouth but froze.

"I know why you came back home," she continued, voice low and lethal. "And if you think for one second I'm gonna let you hurt him again... if you think I'm gonna fucking near lose him again because of you... I swear I'll make sure you aren't allowed around him, or anyone he loves, ever again. That means I'll make sure you're not welcome here at Quinn's either."

My throat went dry. I wanted to argue, to explain, to tell her it wasn't like that, that I hadn't meant for anything to happen.

But Lena didn't care. When it came to Ash, she didn't fuck around.

Before I could respond, Quinn's voice cut through the tension, careful but loud enough to break the edge.

"Hey... everything okay out here?"

She stepped outside, stunning as always.

I glanced at her, then back at Lena. The fury in Lena's eyes didn't soften, didn't falter.

Quinn took a cautious step closer, sensing the hostility between us, like she could almost taste it.

"It's fine," Lena said. But it wasn't fine. Her words were fire in my chest. "Just making sure Sloane understands the rules. One wrong move, one stupid mistake, and I swear—you won't just lose his trust. You'll lose every door you think you're welcome in. Got it?"

I couldn't answer. I didn't have words strong enough to fight her, fast enough to match her. My hands were shaking around the blunt. The smoke wrapped around me like a veil I wanted to hide behind. I wanted to flip shit, go off the handle, tell her to go fuck herself. But I couldn't. Because she was right. The guilt of how I had ripped him apart weighed so heavy on me, I thought my chest would collapse.

Quinn's eyes flicked between us, tense, unsure.

"Hey, we don't have to do this," she said softly. "Let's just... calm down."

Calm? There was no calm. Not here, not with Lena. Her words pressed into me like a warning and a promise at once, and I could feel it curling around my ribs, making my heart pound and my stomach twist.

I wanted to disappear, to run, to hide... but I didn't. I could only stand there, smoke stinging my lungs, and take what she was dishing out. Take every cold, cutting word and let it sink.

I opened my mouth, words scrambling, but all that came out was a sharp, flustered, "I... I'm not—"

Lena's eyes narrowed, icy as ever, but I couldn't stop myself. Something in me snapped, a little spark of temper flaring.

"Look, I'm not here to—"

Quinn immediately stepped between us, eyes wide, muscles tensed like she could physically hold Lena back.

"Hey—enough," she said, voice tight, clearly on edge.

I clenched my jaw, hands still shaking from the smoke and adrenaline, but I bit back, my words coming faster, sharper than I meant:

"I didn't mean to hurt him! I'm not—God, I'm not some heartless bitch, okay? And Ash ain't no fuckin' saint either!"

Quinn's hands flexed at her sides. "Sloane—" she warned, but I couldn't stop myself.

Lena's glare didn't budge, and I added, "I'm not the enemy here, Lena. Neither of us were innocent!"

The words hit the air like fire, and I saw Quinn flinch. Her eyes darted between us, heart racing, shoulders stiff. Lena's mouth pressed into a thin line, jaw tight.

Finally, Quinn grabbed her arm. "Enough!" she snapped, dragging Lena back a step. "Come on, we're late for dinner. Let's go."

Dinner? Already? I thought, stunned. I'd literally spent all day glued to my phone, texting Ash like an idiot. Impossible.

Lena muttered under her breath as Quinn steered her away, but I didn't hear the words. I watched them go, heart still racing, and turned back inside.

I grabbed a snack, fumbling for something to eat while trying to calm my pulse.

Then my phone buzzed in my back pocket.

Heart hammering again, pulse spiking, I pulled it out, expecting – hoping – it wasn't Ash.

It wasn't. Thank God.

Kassidy.

Hey babe, wanna have a drink tonight?

Chapter 35

I went to the little bar downtown that Kassidy and I had first met at, grabbing a drink at the bar before walking to the patio in the back to where Kassidy was.

"Bout damn time" Kassidy said winking at me as I sat down next to her. I took a sip of my drink as my phone dinged.

Ash.

You're playing with fire if you're with anyone other than me, Sloane... why you wanna do this to yourself? You know whatever game you're playing, I can play better.

How the hell did he always know? My chest tightened, anger and heat colliding in my veins.

Good. Let him burn.

I shoved the phone into my back pocket and turned back to Kassidy, grabbing her by the hoodie and kissing her like I meant to wipe Ash off my tongue.

"Whoa," she laughed against my mouth, breathless.

"Take me to your place," I demanded.

Her brows shot up, then she grinned slow. "Your wish."

I barely recalled the walk there; we were in such a hurry.

By the time we got there, I was buzzing – from the liquor, from Ash's words still haunting me, from Lena's threat, from the ache between my legs that no text could quiet.

Kassidy shut the door, and I had her pressed against it in a second, hands in her hair, mouth hot and hard.

"Bedroom," she gasped.

We stumbled in, clothes hitting the floor in a trail behind us. Kassidy's room looked like a playground for sinners – cuffs on the headboard, a swing hanging from the ceiling, toys lined up like weapons on her dresser.

"Jesus," I breathed, pulse spiking.

"Pick, I've been waiting for our next chance together." she said simply, smirking.

I grabbed the butterfly vibrator again, but Kassidy wasn't done – she pulled out a pair of leather cuffs, snapping them around my wrists before I could second-guess.

"Trust me?" she asked.

I nodded.

"Good girl."

The words made my stomach flip.

Minutes later, I was strapped into the swing, spread wide and helpless while the vibrator pressed against my clit, buzzing low. Kassidy teased me until I was squirming, dragging her nails along my thighs, kissing everywhere but where I needed.

"Please," I panted.

She turned the vibrator up a notch. "Beg for it."

My hips jerked. "Please, Kassidy–fuck, please."

That got her. She knelt between my legs, licking slow, deep, letting me ride the edge until I was gasping.

Then she grabbed the double-ended dildo, sliding one end into herself with a groan, the other pushing into me until we were connected. She started moving slow, rocking the swing, each thrust hitting deeper, wetter, the toy vibrating against my clit sending sparks up my spine.

"God—fuck—" I cried, gripping the ropes so hard my arms shook.

Kassidy leaned forward, sucking my nipple into her mouth, grinding harder until we were both moaning, both right there, on the edge.

"Say my name," she ordered, breath hot against my skin.

"Kassidy—oh God—"

"Louder."

"KASSIDY!"

She grinned against my chest and pumped harder, faster, until I shattered around her, screaming, my body jerking in the swing.

But she didn't stop.

She flipped me, unstrapped me, bent me over the edge of the bed, and slid the toy back inside me from behind, fingers circling my clit while she fucked me until I was crying, legs trembling, begging her to stop and not stop at the same time.

When I came again, it was harder, messier, the orgasm tearing through me until I collapsed face-first on the bed.

I thought we were done.

She laughed low. "Not yet."

She straddled my thigh, grinding, and I let her use me, let her come hard against my leg, slick soaking my skin.

Ash's words came back like a slap:

You're playing with fire if you're with anyone other than me, Sloane... whatever game you're playing, I can play better.

Something in me snapped.

I grabbed Kassidy by the hips and flipped her onto her back, my breath coming in hot, ragged bursts.

"Oh, fuck," she gasped, but I was already climbing on top of her, already forcing my thigh between hers, pinning her down.

"You think you get to finish on me and be done?" My voice was low, dangerous. Maybe I was talking to her. Maybe I was talking to him.

She moaned, eyes wide. "Sloane—"

"Not another word.."

I ground down against her, wet against wet, hard enough to make the bed frame squeal. The dildo was still inside us, buried deep, rubbing with every grind so that our clits were smashing together, slippery and hot.

Kassidy grabbed the sheets, head thrown back, whimpering as I rode her mercilessly, using her body like it was mine.

Ash's voice echoed in my head with every thrust – *I can play better.*

"Oh yeah?" I hissed through my teeth, dragging her knee up over my shoulder so I could angle deeper, faster, making sure the toy stayed stuffed inside us both. "Watch me."

Her breath hitched. "Oh my god—"

"Yeah, you feel that?" I gritted, grinding harder, our clits rubbing together in wet, messy circles. "You're gonna cum when I tell you."

She was whimpering, close to tears, nails clawing at my back.

"Cum for me," I demanded, voice sharp as a whip.

She shattered beneath me, screaming, body shaking, and I didn't stop – I rode it out, chasing my own release like I was trying to erase him from my skin.

When I came, it was violent, my orgasm tearing through me until I was nearly sobbing.

I collapsed beside her, both of us shaking, slick and sweat everywhere, the dildo sliding out of us.

Kassidy just stared at me, wrecked and wide-eyed.

And all I could think was –
Game on, Ash.

As my body collapsed against hers, slick and trembling, my phone buzzed in my jeans on the floor. I reached down and fumbled it out of my pocket as Kassidy ran her fingers over my bare back.

I knew before I looked.

Ash.

Saw what you did, Sloane. Naughty girl. I told you what it would be being with anyone other than me.

Heat and fury coiled in my stomach. My fingers clenched the sheets. He knew. Of course he knew. He always had a way of knowing. But he damn sure didn't see shit.

I texted back.
You don't know shit, Ash.

I froze. His words weren't just teasing – they were venomous. Sharp. His voice echoed in my head, the one I couldn't escape: *I can play better.*

I swallowed hard. Rage and desire tangled inside me, making my pulse stutter. I wanted to throw the phone, I wanted to call him, I wanted to drag him here and shove his smug grin into the floor, while forcing him to watch me fuck someone who wasn't him.

Instead... I gritted my teeth and typed back again, slow:

Game on.

The reply was instant, as though he'd been waiting:

Good. I like a challenge.

I tossed the phone to the foot of the bed, heart hammering, sweat dripping, body still shaking.

I laid back against Kassidy, slick skin, soaked sheets. And I knew – no matter what I did tonight, Ash's shadow was still on me, and he was going to make me pay.

My phone buzzed again. My breath hitched.

Ash.

My chest tightened, but it wasn't a message; it was a photo.

The image hit me like a punch: Ash, bare chest, covered in tattoos, all sharp edges, sprawled in his bed. One muscled arm slung casually over the naked woman curled into him, sheet barely covering her. His other hand was holding the phone, aimed down at them, his smirk carved into place like he knew exactly what he was doing to me.

I told you I could play better.

My stomach flipped. Rage and jealousy flared so fast it made me dizzy.

My thumb hovered, white-knuckled, over the screen. I wanted to throw the phone, shatter it, scream.

Instead, I forced myself to breathe, even though it felt like glass ripping down my throat.

Because if Ash thought this would break me? He was absolutely fucking right.

Chapter 36

The next morning Kassidy drove us in a comfortable silence, the kind that felt easy after the chaos of the night before. My fingers twined in hers on the center console, the warmth grounding me.

"Babe, something on your mind?" she asked finally, glancing at me from the corner of her eye. Her thumb brushed my knuckles, gentle.

"Yea but it's not something I like to talk about," I muttered, though I wasn't entirely sure I didn't want to spill my guts to her about my dangerous fascination with Ash and the bullshit he brings. My body was still buzzing from last night, still tangled in fire and want, but her presence calmed some of the chaos. I didn't want to ruin that. Not right now.

She smiled, soft, teasing. "Okay... So... when will I see you again?"

I smirked, letting the corner of my lips twitch. "Don't tempt me."

Her laugh filled the car, light and warm, and I had to fight a shiver as I remembered just how good she'd made me feel. "I like being tempted," she whispered, her voice dipping just enough to make my pulse thrum.

We drove in easy conversation after that – small talk about work, music, nothing heavy, just grounding myself in something normal for a few minutes. But it wasn't enough to keep my mind off him. Ash's messages still burned in the back of my skull, each one a reminder that I was never really free.

That picture of him wrapped up in another female that wasn't me haunting my every fuckin' thought. *I told you I can play better.* His message still burned into my mind.

Before long, we pulled up to Quinn's place. My stomach twisted, nervousness bubbling up again. I hadn't seen Lena since last night, and the thought of facing her – or Quinn – made my pulse spike in a different way.

"I hope I see you again soon, babe ," Kassidy said, parking the car for me to get out. "Be safe, okay?"

I nodded, grabbing my bag and slid out of the car. She leaned over, brushing her lips against my cheek. "Text me when you get inside," she said softly.

"I will," I whispered, watching her pull back, giving me one last, lingering smile before she started the car.

I stepped onto the driveway, bag on my shoulder, and just as Kassidy's little blue Convertible Mustang roared to life and started pulling away, my chest tightened.

And that's when I saw her. Lena.

I swallowed hard, my chest tight. And I knew – nothing about today was going to be simple. Hell, nothing in my life ever is.

She'd just stepped outside, and the second her eyes caught the Mustang, they went wide.

Shock, maybe even something darker, flickered across her face. Her jaw tightened, a flash of anger or jealousy – I couldn't tell – before she spun on her heel and stormed back inside.

My stomach twisted. Did she see Kassidy in the car? Did she know? I hadn't told her. I hadn't told anyone.

Every step toward the house felt heavy, my mind racing. What if she saw me with Kassidy last night? My pulse started hammering in my ears, heat crawling up my neck as a dozen ugly possibilities rushed through my head.

By the time I passed Quinn's bedroom door, I froze. Voices.

Lena's sharp, hushed tone filtered through the crack, low and urgent.

"...not okay with this, Quinn—"
"...Kassidy—and Sloane—"

My stomach twisted again at the sound of my own name. How the hell did she even know about Kassidy? How did she know her name even?

I bolted into my room, shutting the door softly behind me, pressing my back against it, breath coming hard. Rage burned jagged and hot, humiliation clawed at my chest, paranoia licked at my skull like fire. My pulse was a drum in my ears, heartbeat echoing in every nerve ending.

Then my phone buzzed.

Ash.

I didn't want to look. I knew I shouldn't. But my hands moved anyway, trembling, fingers hovering over the screen like I was about to touch something poisonous.

I couldn't tear my eyes away from the video Ash had sent me. Dante Santero, sprawled out on the *Underground* ring floor, Ash raining down blow after brutal blow. Blood, sweat, the crowd screaming – but I couldn't hear it. All I could hear was my own heartbeat, thundering, pulsing in my skull.

Ash's text crawled across the screen:
See what happens when you play with fire, Sloane.

Not a threat to me. A warning. To anyone foolish enough to step close. To anyone who dared touch what belonged to him.

I couldn't breathe. My hands shook, fingers clutching the phone like it was the only thing keeping me tethered to the world. Rage burned in my chest, twisting into a heat that was impossible to control. Lust pooled low, dark and sharp, tangled with fear and obsession. I hated him. I wanted him. I feared him. And somehow, I needed him more than air.

I leaned back against the wall, letting my head drop, eyes still locked on Dante's bloodied face. Years ago, that was someone I had touched, someone I had cared about. And Ash had erased him without hesitation. Without a second thought.

Another buzz. Another message.
Don't forget – I always know.

I gritted my teeth, lips pressed tight. My mind was spiraling. Rage. Lust. Fear. Obsession. All of it tangled together into a mess I couldn't untangle.

And in that mess, one thought screamed louder than the rest:
This isn't over. Not for me. Not for anyone.

I threw the phone onto the bed, hands trembling, and ran my fingers through my hair. I needed something normal. Something safe. Something that didn't involve Ash, Dante, or the firestorm this had lit around me.

I grabbed my phone again, dialing Colt before I could second-guess myself.

"Hey," I said when he answered, my voice tight but steady. "You... think we could have dinner tonight? I need... twin time. And honestly, I just need to talk."

There was no hesitation in his voice, just that calm, grounding tone I trusted. "Of course, Lo. Want to come over tonight? Elise has roast cooking in the crock pot."

A small, grateful smile tugged at my lips. "Yeah... that sounds perfect."

"Good. See you then," he said, and I hung up, feeling some of the tension in my chest ease – just a little. Not completely. But enough that I could breathe.

I shoved my phone into my bag and stared out the window, the city below buzzing, oblivious, while my world was anything but. Tonight, at least, I had a place to breathe. A place to be Sloane, not just a pawn in Ash's twisted game.

I knew – the fire wasn't gone. And it would follow me everywhere.

Quinn's apartment was quiet, but my mind was anything but. Tomorrow was the first day back to work since I left California – my first day at AnchorPoint Refuge – and I had to pull my shit together.

I unpacked my bag, laying out clothes for the morning: a baby blue blouse that said "professional" but didn't scream stiffness, blue skinny jeans that let me move without feeling trapped, shoes that wouldn't make me wince halfway through the day. Each piece felt like armor, a small attempt at control in a life that had been anything but.

I checked my notes for the first client sessions, carefully reviewing case files, reading up on trauma-centered strategies, grounding techniques. My fingers lingered over the pages, but my thoughts kept slipping. Ash. Dante. Kassidy. Lena. The fire Ash had lit with that video still burned in my chest, and I could feel the heat in my palms even as I wrote notes.

Coffee in hand, I paced the living room. Quinn's apartment felt too quiet now – every creak, every hum of electricity made my stomach twist. Quinn and Lena were both at work. Quinn at the hospital as a CNA. Lena at Walker Customs, working with Ash on the motorcycles.

I didn't look at my phone. I couldn't. Ash's shadow was probably lurking there, waiting to remind me that nothing in my world was safe.

I set a few small things out: my notebook, pens, a calming essential-oil blend on the nightstand – lavender to settle my mind, peppermint to keep me sharp. Tiny things for normalcy, for focus, for pretending that tomorrow I'd be Sloane, not just a target in the fucked-up game Ash and I neither one knew how to stop playing.

You'd think I'd know better. I help people survive, pick up the pieces, teach them how to breathe when the world shatters – and here I am, shattering anyway, and shattering Ash too, because we just never stop ruining each other.

Ash. Fucking Ash. With him there are no rules, no lines, no

sense, no corner of safety anywhere. I push, I shove, I tell myself to quit, to walk, to just stop, and yet my hands twitch like they're reaching for him anyway. My chest twists, my stomach flips, my blood hums. I can't quit him. I can't quit us. I can't quit the fire, the madness, the pull that makes me ache, makes me burn, makes me want him even when I hate him, even when I know it's nothing but poison. And maybe the worst part is that I don't even want to quit.

By the time it was time to head over to Colt's, I'd rehearsed my first day of work at AnchorPoint a dozen ways in my head. What I'd say to clients, how I'd hold my own, how I'd keep the fire outside my door. And yet... it didn't feel enough.

I got out of the shower towel wrapped around me, looking in my closet for something to wear when my phone buzzed again.

I froze and turned around to see my phone on my bed with the screen lit up, Ash's name burning back at me.

Three words. Just three.

Wear red tonight.

My stomach dropped, the floor tilting beneath me, breath catching somewhere between terror and hunger.

I should block him. I should throw the phone. I should do anything but what I knew I'd do next.

I opened my closet.

And reached for red.

Chapter 37

As I headed to Colt's, my fingers were tight around the steering wheel, knuckles white, heart hammering as I thought about what I was about to do – sit across from Colt and tell him about Ash. Try to explain this thing between us that made no sense and hurt like hell but wouldn't let me go.

And then, like some cruel trick, my brain decided to snap me back to a time that made my face flush.

In a camper bathroom at a campground during a weekend getaway. Ash had me bent over the bathroom sink, my cheek nearly pressed to the cold counter, my breath fogging the mirror as he slammed into me from behind. My fingers gripped the porcelain so hard my knuckles ached. His tattooed hand was over my mouth, muffling every cry he was dragging out of me.

"Fuck, you're so wet for me," he rasped against my ear, and I caught his grin in the mirror – that infuriating, dimpled grin that always meant trouble.

The mirror shook with every thrust, the little bathroom filled with the sound of skin against skin, my choked whimpers, his breathless curses. Then–

BANG BANG BANG.

"The fuck is going on in there? Sloane, open the door!"

Ash didn't slow down. If anything, he went harder, hips snapping against me, making the counter dig into my stomach with each brutal thrust. The mirror clattered against the wall, my moans spilling out louder, no longer muffled, no longer controlled. Colt's pounding shook the door, the knob rattling like it might break.

"Don't act like I don't know what y'all are doing! Open this FUCKING door!" Colt's voice thundered through the door as he

continued to beat on it.

Instead of stopping, Ash laughed – the cocky bastard – and went harder, driving me into the counter with every stroke. My eyes rolled back, the mix of fear and adrenaline sending me spiraling straight into orgasm. I bit down on his hand to keep from screaming as Colt's pounding grew louder, the knob rattling like he was about to rip the door off it's hinges.

"I swear to God–"

Ash pulled out just in time, biting back another laugh as I dropped my skirt back down and grabbed my toothbrush pretending to be brushing my teeth. My legs still trembled as Colt finally shoved the door open. He froze, glaring between us. Ash was sitting on the toilet with his head in his hands like he'd just sat down to take a shit, playing it off so damn calm it almost broke me. Like he hadn't just made me cum so hard I could barely stand, floor still soaked from the proof. Colt glaring daggers into us.

My chest still heaved by the time I turned down Colt's street, my body thrumming like Ash was still behind me, still inside me, still grinning at me in that damn mirror.

I hated that the memory still had claws in me, that my body still buzzed like I hadn't just been wrecked by it. That heat between my legs? Not just from shame. The awkwardness that moment caused was still fresh in my mind.

Colt knew. No doubt at all that he knew what went down in that camper.

By the time I parked outside Colt's, I'd convinced myself I could hold it together. Or at least fake it 'til I make it.

Colt and Elise were easy enough to talk to at first, filling the air with light conversation. But the second Ash's name came up, my chest tightened.

And just like that, I was back there – later that night after Colt had caught us in the bathroom.

"Look," he'd said, his voice low and steady, "I see the way you've looked at each other. I can tell there isn't gonna be a way to stop it. So I'm going to give y'all the green light — but don't get it twisted. I damn sure don't approve. The way y'all mind-fuck each other is insane. You both run from what you really feel and I've never seen a more ridiculous game."

Ash had been standing there, jaw tight, still deep in denial. And I hadn't said a word, because Colt was right — and we all knew it.

The memory made my chest ache, and I dragged in a deep breath before blurting it out.

"Colt... it's still toxic as hell between me and Ash," I admitted, my voice low but sharp. "I thought leaving would fix things, but I couldn't let him go. So I thought maybe coming back would fix it — but it hasn't. If anything, it's worse.

"At least when I moved on with Cage, he couldn't hurt him — because you and Quinn kept where I was a secret. But I'm back now, and Ash is being ridiculous. He hurt Dante, bad. And he did it just to prove a point."

"You're his best friend C-Bear — you have to talk to him. Tell him to chill the fuck out before this gets completely out of control," I pleaded.

Colt blew out a slow breath, dragging a hand down his face. "Jesus, Lo," he muttered. "You really think he listens to me anymore? He's half-feral where you're concerned. But yeah... I'll say something. Somebody's gotta keep him from burning the whole damn world down over you."

Colt's words sat heavy between us, filling the room like smoke.

"Thank you," I said finally, voice barely above a whisper.

Colt leaned forward, elbows on his knees, eyes hard. "Listen to me, Sloane — if he lays another hand on someone just to get to you, I will put him on his ass. I don't care if he's my best friend. I don't care. You come first, Lo. Always."

That promise hit me like a punch to the gut. Elise reached over, squeezing my knee — a quiet show of solidarity — but my chest still felt like it was collapsing in on itself.

Because if I knew anything about Ash, it was that a warning like that wouldn't scare him. It would just light him up. Even if it was his best friend giving that warning.

And as I stepped out into the cool night air, I knew, without a doubt, that surviving what Ash had planned next would take everything I had — and then some.

Chapter 38

I stood in front of my closet, staring at the boring red shirt I'd worn earlier to Colt's.

Ash's words echoed in my head – *wear red* – and for a second, I wanted to rebel, to make a point and put on anything but.

My pulse kicked up. If I was going to do this, I was going to make him pay for telling me what to do. So instead, I went all in.

Since Colt had gone and gotten my things from California, I now had my entire wardrobe. I pulled out the red dress – the one I swore I'd never wear around Ash because it clung to every curve and left nothing to the imagination. It slid over my skin like it was made for me. The mirror didn't lie – it hugged my hips, showed off just enough cleavage to be dangerous, and stopped just short of indecent.

My heart thudded as I twisted my hair up, swiped on lipstick that matched the dress, and stepped back to take myself in.

Ash wasn't ready for this.

My phone buzzed.

I'll be there at 8. Be ready.

I smiled to myself – oh, I was ready.

The rumble of his Harley came right on time, vibrating through my chest before I even stepped outside.

When I walked out, his head snapped up – and there it was, that grin. The one that said he'd already won.

"Holy shit," he muttered, dimples flashing.

I didn't say a word, just swung a leg over the bike, letting the skirt of the dress ride dangerously high as I settled behind him. His laugh rumbled low in his chest as we tore off into the night.

The rooftop was unreal. Fairy lights strung between beams, candles flickering on every table, the whole city glittering around us. Couples sat close together, their voices blending with music and clinking glasses.

Ash didn't sit across from me – he slid into the chair right next to mine, thigh brushing mine like he belonged there.

He leaned in, lips brushing my ear. "Remember that night at Quinn's years ago?" he murmured.

"That fancy Christmas dinner with Colt and Lena – you sitting right next to me in that tiny dress? How I had my hand under the table, fingers so deep in you you could barely breathe?"

His grin curved slow, cocky, dimples deep. "Colt knew. Hell, Lena probably did too. I still remember the way your leg kicked when you came all over my fingers, trying so hard not to make a sound."

My breath caught.

"Oh no," I muttered, because I knew that grin. My eyes went wide, and his smile just spread wider, like he'd been waiting for this moment all night.

Ash ordered for us – steak for him, salad for me – he knows me so well.

"Bourbon, neat," he said, then nodded at me. "And a bourbon mix for her. She loves the girlie shit." He laughed as I rolled my eyes.

When the waiter left, the hum of conversation filled the space – music buzzing, glasses clinking, soft laughter from other tables.

And then Ash's hand slid onto my knee.

At first it was casual. Innocent.

Then it wasn't.

Then his thumb drew lazy circles, fingers trailing higher until they slipped beneath the slit in my dress.

My breath hitched, my thighs tensing.

"You're insane," I whispered, gripping my glass until the ice clinked against the sides.

His grin deepened. "And you love it."

His fingers kept climbing, sliding over the thin lace of my panties until they were right where I ached for him. My breath caught, heat rushing to my face.

"Don't," I hissed.

"Then tell me to stop."

I didn't. Couldn't.

He pushed the lace aside and dragged his fingers through me, slow, like he had all the time in the world.

I bit the inside of my cheek hard, pretending to sip my drink as pleasure shot straight through me.

"Fuck, Sloane," he murmured, low and rough. "You're soaked already."

I swallowed hard, staring out at the skyline while his fingers slipped inside me, his thumb circling until my whole body trembled.

Around us, people laughed, forks scraped against plates, glasses clinked. No one knew.

And that made it so much worse.

—or better.

While I kept my face perfectly blank for anyone who might be watching.

Ash didn't move his hand. He kept stroking me through it, slow and filthy, until I was shaking.

"Ash—" I choked, my nails digging into his thigh.

"Be quiet," he murmured, mouth brushing my temple. "Or I'll make you scream."

His pace quickened, fingers curling just right, and I broke – biting my lip hard enough to taste copper, my whole body shaking as I came, silent and raw, under the table.

Ash didn't stop right away. He kept stroking me slow, drawing every last wave out of me until I had to grab his wrist to make him stop while still trying to keep a blank face.

It was damn near impossible.

When he finally pulled back, he brought his fingers to his mouth, sucking them clean with a satisfied hum.

"Goddamn," he said softly, leaning close enough that only I could hear. "You're mine tonight, Sloane. Every fucking part of you."

I was still shaking when the waiter came back with our food.

Ash acted like nothing happened – cut into his steak, poured the wine, took a sip. His calm made it worse. My pulse hadn't even slowed.

He passed me my glass, his smirk deepening when our fingers brushed.

"You're quiet," he said casually.

I shot him a look, cheeks still hot.

He smirked, "Eat," he said. "You're gonna need the energy later."

I glared at him, cheeks still flushed, knees still buzzing under the table, but I picked up my fork anyway.

We ate, and he didn't let me relax. Every brush of his thigh against mine, every casual graze of his fingers along my hand made me ache. But I had to play it cool – pretend like I wasn't already undone.

After dinner, he grabbed my hand, tugging me toward the small space left for dancing. "Come on," he said, his grin cocky, dimples deep.

"I don't dance, you know this," I muttered.

"Lucky for you, I do," he shot back, spinning me close, pressing me to him.

The music throbbed softly around us, candles flickering. His hand settled at my waist, pulling me against him, and I let the tension slip into something dangerous, addictive. Every step, every sway of his hips against mine made my pulse spike, made my body remember every time he'd touched me, teased me, held me, driven me crazy.

We laughed when he nearly stepped on my heels. I joked back, teasing him about his reckless dancing. He laughed, that deep, low sound that made my stomach clench and my knees weak.

His eyes glimmered, dark and dangerous, and I knew he could see every thought racing through my mind.

We spun around the small rooftop, the city lights sparkling beneath us, the stars above.

Cocky, impossible, completely reckless – him laughing, me laughing, teasing, dancing, the tension between us crackling like fire.

Then he whispered, brushing my hair back from my face, voice low: "Let's get out of here."

Before I could protest, he was grabbing his keys off the table, dragging me by the hand through the doors and down the stairs.

The Harley roared to life as Ash got on and kicked his kickstand up, and I threw myself onto the back of it, holding on tight around his waist. Wind whipped my hair around my face, the city blurring past us, the thrill of speed and danger twisting in my chest.

The ride was a rush — adrenaline, lust, and the lingering heat of dinner still pressing between us. I pressed closer to him, the smell of leather and his cologne intoxicating, and I felt him smile against my temple.

We stepped inside Ash's house. The warmth from the night still clung to me, my blood still buzzing from dancing, from him.

"Knox," Ash muttered, his eyes flicking toward the massive pit bull barreling toward us. Muscle and teeth and sheer presence, Knox's growl rumbled through the room.

"I'll feed him," Ash said, heading for the kitchen, Knox padding behind him.

That's when I saw it — his phone lighting up on the counter with the name Vanessa sprawled across it. Before he even realized, I snatched it. My hands shaking, heart hammering.

I miss the way you taste.

The words burned in me.

"And this is why I don't fucking let you in..." I said slow and disgusted. "This is why I don't fucking trust you—"

Ash spun around, confusion written all over his face. "Sloane... what—what's wrong? What do you mean?"

"You will never stop breaking me," I whispered, handing him his phone as he looked down at the message. A look of panic crept over him.

"No, Sloane, it's not what you think–"

"Righhhhtttt." I laughed, the sound sharp, insane, the psycho switch flipping hard. "You're not gonna really try to lie your way out of this, Ash, are you?" His eyes showed a flash of intense irritation.

"You don't get to do this, Sloane! You don't get to play victim after how you up and ran out on me – after I bared everything to you!"

I took a step toward him, jaw tight. "Oh, please! You faked that too – just like you faked tonight–"

"Sloane, that's a goddamn lie!!"

"Oh, please! Go have fun with Vanessa. Or Ember. Or whoever. 'Cause Sloane Motherfuckin' Carter is DONE!"

"Yes, 'cause you're a saint, Sloane. You left. You got engaged to someone that wasn't me. And that fuckin' destroyed me!"

Ash went quiet, like the weight of it hit him for a second.

"Don't turn this around, Ash," I said, voice low but deadly. "Call Vanessa. I'm done. This is goodbye."

I stormed to the front door, slamming it behind me. The cold night air hit me like a punch, Knox barking behind the glass, Ash's shout echoing after me, but I didn't look back.

Not this time.

Chapter 39

I fumbled for my phone as I stepped onto the curb, my fingers trembling. Quinn. Of course. She'd pick me up. She always did.

She arrived a few minutes later, her familiar jeep rumbling up like a lifeline. I slid into the passenger seat, heart still hammering, and she didn't ask questions – not yet. She just drove.

The ride home was quiet, the kind of silence that isn't empty but full of unspoken understanding. I kept my gaze fixed on the streetlights passing by, pretending I wasn't shaking from adrenaline, anger, and a heat I couldn't begin to sort out.

When I got inside, the smell of Lena's perfume hit me first. She was in bed, already asleep, and Quinn guided me to the living room without a word. She curled up on the couch, patting the spot next to her.

"Talk to me," she said softly.

I let out a shaky laugh. "Where do I even start?"

She tilted her head, eyes searching mine. "Start with what's in your heart. I can handle it, I've got you regardless."

I swallowed, the weight of the night pressing down. "Ash... he's... he's like nothing I've ever known. He gets under my skin. He makes me feel... everything, all at once. I thought it was gonna work out this time just like I get that same little bit of hope like every other time....and this motherfucker has the bitch he sent me a pic of in his bed the other night, texting him."

Quinn's brow furrowed and she let our a big sigh. "I get it. I really do. But Sloane... he's dangerous. Not just the way he touches you or mind fucks you – it's more than that. He'll consume you if you let him. Look at what he's already doing to you."

"I know," I whispered, my hands twisting in my lap. "I know he's reckless. That he's... consuming. But I can't–"

"No." Quinn cut me off gently. "You can't let him. Not like this. You're smart. You're strong. You've survived everything he's thrown at you so far. But if you let him in completely, if you let yourself drown in him... it'll wreck you in a whole new way. You'll lose yourself, Sloane. And I won't let that happen."

I swallowed hard, staring down at my shaking hands. "I don't know if I can stay away," I admitted, my voice raw. "I keep thinking about him... every touch, every word. It's like he's... everywhere. Its like we are meant to be no matter how fucked up it gets."

Quinn reached out, her hand brushing mine, grounding me. "Then you let me be your anchor. Let me help you hold onto yourself. You don't have to do this alone, Sloane. You're allowed to fight for you – not just get lost in him again."

The words settled over me, a mix of comfort and warning. I wanted to resist, to run back to him, to let the fire consume me. But Quinn's steady gaze, the way she wasn't judging me, just holding space for me... it made me realize something.

I had a choice. And for once, I could fight against the pull of Ash Walker.

I leaned back against the couch, Quinn's presence like a shield. "Okay," I whispered. "Okay. I'll try. I'll... try to keep myself together."

She smiled, small but fierce, and squeezed my hand.

"Can I talk to you about something else?" Quinn asked, her voice tight, clearly nervous.

I frowned, tilting my head. "Absolutely."

"Who's this girl you've been hanging out with? Or... is it more than that? What is that?"

"Kassidy?" I asked, unsure where this was going.

Quinn just stared at me, eyes wide, and I felt the unease settle deeper in my chest.

"I've... I've slept with her a couple times," I admitted, voice low. "I'm not really sure what it is exactly. All I know is she's not Ash. Why?"

Her mouth dropped open, eyes huge. "Lo... do you not know who that woman is?"

I blinked, confusion pressing at me. "What do you mean?"

Before she could answer, Lena barreled into the room, cheerful as ever. "Hey, you coming to bed, babe?"

"Yeah, I'm coming," Quinn said quickly. She turned to me, her expression softening just slightly. "Sloane... get some sleep, hun. I'll talk to you tomorrow." She got up, heading toward her room – Quinn and Lena disappearing behind the door.

What did she mean by that? I wondered, heart thumping. My mind raced, imagining a million scenarios, none of them good.

I shrugged off the tension as best I could, grabbing a loose T-shirt and my underwear before heading to the bathroom. The water from the shower ran hot, steaming against the glass, and I let it hit my skin, trying to wash away Ash's touch – the lingering heat and ache that had me trembling still.

Every droplet felt like it carried a memory – the stolen touches under the table, the way he'd made me melt with just a look – and I closed my eyes, pressing my forehead against the cool tile, willing it all away.

But no matter how hard I tried, I could feel it: him. Ash. Every pulse, every nerve ending still alive with his presence.

I hated it, but I couldn't deny it.

I stepped out, wrapping a towel around myself. I rubbed my hair dry, avoiding the mirror for a moment, trying not to see Ash's smug grin flashing back at me. But of course, I seen it anyway – in every reflection, in the ghost of every touch.

I pulled on my T-shirt and underwear, feet dragging as I padded back to my room. The house was quiet, the only sound the faint hum of the city outside. I sat on the edge of my bed, hugging my knees, trying to make sense of the tangle in my chest.

Quinn's words echoed. *Do you not know who that woman is?* Her panic, the way she'd stared at me wide eyed... it made no sense.

I wanted to go in there and wake her up, demand she explain. But I didn't. I couldn't. Not yet. And honestly, part of me was afraid of the answer.

And then there was Ash. That night. That entire night. Every touch, every tease, every filthy, possessive whisper. It was like he'd burned himself into my skin, my mind, and my body refused to let him go – and then ripped my heart from my chest just like every time before.

I pressed my face into the pillow, the scent of my own shampoo mingling with the lingering heat in my blood, wishing I could scrub him out of me. But I couldn't. I couldn't even pretend I wanted to.

I rolled onto my back, staring at the ceiling, heart still racing. Quinn was right. If I let Ash back in completely, he would consume me. He'd take every piece of me and twist it until I was no longer Sloane. And yet... even thinking of keeping him at arm's length felt impossible.

I squeezed my eyes shut, trying to hold onto the part of me that was mine alone – the part Quinn had reminded me to protect. The part that could survive this... that could survive him.

My phone buzzed next to my head. Heart pounding, I picked it up.

No more games. We do this for real.

Fuck you, Ash Walker.

Sleep came slow, tangled with worry, desire, and the faintest thread of fear. Tomorrow, I promised myself, I'd stop loving him. Tomorrow, I'd start figuring it out. Tomorrow, maybe, I could start being just Sloane again.

But tonight... tonight, Ash still haunted me, and there was no escaping him. There never would be.

Chapter 40

I couldn't sleep. Kept tossing and turning, my mind unraveling with the worry I had for Sloane. I was making myself sick.

I knew what Ash did to her every damn time. There was a reason that she moved to California and swore me and Colt to secrecy. That was the only way she could escape him and that damn hold he had on her and Colt and I both knew it.

I thought I had betrayed Sloane when I let it slip to Lena that Sloane was in California. I hadn't meant to.

Lena walked in the back door, completely distraught, on the verge of tears, looking beyond defeated.

"Babe what's wrong?" I asked, crossing the distance between us in a matter of seconds and wrapping her up into my arms.

"I just left Walkers Customs...It's Ash. He looked Sloane up on Facebook. She's engaged." Lena's eyes were huge, almost as if begging me to tell her it wasn't true.

"Yes...she told me two nights ago. Cage asked her to marry him." I said quietly.

Anger flashed in Lena's eyes. "Nobody fuckin' understands what the hell that's going to do to him, Quinn! I'm so sick of that bitch having that hold on him! I'm so sick of him worshipping her just to get his goddamn heart ripped out!"

She had tears streaming down her face as she slammed her fist down on the table.

"She went to Cali to escape, Lena. She left so they couldn't continue tearing each other apart." I wrapped my arms around her again

holding her as she sobbed in my arms.

"She moved to Cali?" She pushed out of my grasp.

I remember hesitating because nobody was suppose to know that. Especially anybody with connection to Ash. Slowly I shook my head looking down, ready to shove my own foot into my mouth to keep from saying anything more.

Then BANG, BANG BANG! on my door. My eyes widened as Ash starts screaming to let him in.

I opened the door and Ash comes stumbling in, whiskey strong on his breath.

"I need to see Sloane. I can't fuckin' take it anymore. She can't marry him—she's suppose to be mine!" Words slurring with every syllable as he stumbled toward the couch to sit down with Lena right on his heels, arms out ready to catch him if he lost his balance.

"Well Cali is a little too far, Ash." Lena said helping him sit down. Ash's face tensed, his eyes grew wide and a look of realization crept over his face.

Lena had realized what she had just done and hurried to try to fix the can of warms she just opened.

"Cali..." Ash said quietly and slowly, like still trying to wrap his head around that simple word that changed everything.

"Cali." He said again as clarity hit him. Lena started to panic hearing the tension in his voice.

"Ash..don't go getting ideas. I hadn't meant for that to slip-" Lena started.

"Wait—you fuckin' knew?!?!" Ash asked in disbelief, throwing his hands up, the layer of betrayal hanging heavy in the air.

"I found out tonight." Lena said defeated as Ash started to stand

up from the couch.

"I gotta go find her!" Lena pushed him back down.

Lena became all motherly, as she scolded him like a little kid. "Not tonight you're not. Your'e shit faced drunk and clearly not in the mind set to be going anywhere other than that damn couch, Ash Walker."

I expected Ash to argue, to stand back up and tell Lena he was going anyways. I expected him to be out the door before she could even begin to catch up to him. I was surprised when Ash laid down like Lena had told him to. He closed his eyes and curled his legs up to his chest mumbling Sloane's name over and over again like a prayer on Redemption Day.

Lena walked to the hallway closet and pulled out a blanket and draped it over Ash's trembling body. "Get some sleep, Ash." She said quietly, bending down to kiss his forehead. He didn't even acknowledge it.

"I don't want to leave him like this. I hate what that bitch does to him, Quinn!" Lena's hands were in fists, her knuckles turning white.

"Hey now...remember Sloane isn't just a random, babe. She's my best friend. Just like Ash is your best friend. We need to set a boundary, a line, right now that neither of us can cross when it comes to Ash and Sloane."

Lena shook her head in agreeance as she unclinched her fists. "Your'e right. We have to tread lightly." she agreed quietly at the realization.

"Ash will be fine, babe. He's getting some much needed rest. Let's go to bed too." I grabbed her by the hand and gave a little tug. Her feet were planted, like she wanted to go but she didn't know how to force her feet to move.

"You go ahead and go babe. I'll be there in a bit. I'm just gonna stay with him a while longer." I nodded and then went to bed. It was a few hours later when Lena finally came to bed as well. She woke me up slipping in beside me as she wrapped me in her arms.

The next morning we woke to Ash being gone, A note on the fridge read:

Heading to Cali. Have to find her. Don't worry about me, I'll be okay. Love you.
-Ash
P.S. Thank you.

And let me tell you what, Lena about lost her damn mind. She yelled and cussed and hit the fridge that held his note. She then ripped it off the fridge and ripped it into pieces, hands still shaking, still hella pissed. "Goddamn him! Goddamn that motherfucker!" She was now beating the shit out of the fridge. Each hit-another dent in the chrome.

I stopped her fist mid throw and turned her toward me, forcing her to look into my eyes to calm down.

"He'll be back Lena." I said trying to calm my own heart, pulling her in to wrap my arms around her. I could smell her raspberry velvet shampoo as i breathed in her scent. Lena's shaking finally started to slow to a stop.

I knew what Ash going after Sloane meant. And Sloane would never forgive me if he found her.

I had to hope and pray with everything in me that he didn't have any luck. I'd never forgive myself either. The one and only thing Sloane had ever asked of me our entire friendship, our entire life- was not to tell Ash where she was. And I did exactly that. Well not exactly-but may as well fuckin' have with my big ass mouth.

I swallowed hard, the lump in my throat making it damn near impossible to breathe.

The man left with nothing but his Harley, phone, and the clothes on his back. We only knew he had his phone because him and Lena share a Life360 Circle and that's the first thing she did when she found out he was gone. But yet his stubborn ass wouldn't answer any of Lena's million calls and messages. Which of course only sent her crashing out even harder.

I was cursing him then just like I'm cursing him now. I shook my head as if to shake the memory away. I thought Sloane going to Cali would have been good for her, I thought she would have finally been able to leave his ass in the past where he belonged, once and for all.

But it was almost as if being away from him, only made her want him more. She'd bring him up occasionally when we'd talk when she was away. I'd walk that line very tight. I didn't like talking about him because I hated how I could hear her coming apart at the seams with every word said.

It was torture to watch. Sloane and Ash were the perfect example of star-crossed lovers. They had never loved or wanted somebody so goddamn bad in their lives. So bad that they instantly sabotage the second things are too calm because they don't know how to not destroy each other. It's a never ending cycle. A broken record, stuck on repeat. A car crash you just can't look away from.

Lena rolled over mumbling something about boscos sticks and I smiled. I wish love could be this simple for Sloane. She deserves so much in life. Not to be tied to the ghost of someone who does nothing but rip her heart out, just to put it back together, just to do it all over again- because the first thousand times of her begging me to take the pain away wasn't enough for him.

I wanted so badly for them to make it because they truly are perfect together but the problem is neither one will ever allow it to happen. They'd rather destroy each other and then blame the other while they are both trapped in the blaze, even if it means everyone around them is caught in the crossfire too. And that's what it is—every single time.

I've known Sloane and Colt since they were 4 years old. Our parents use to hang out every day before their parents died. We would either go to their house or they would come to ours. But it was every single day. We grew up being the best friends and still to this day I'd take a bullet for that bitch. She's my soul sister.

When their parents died, Sloane really lost herself. Colt and I had to take turns sitting with her as she was too depressed to be left alone. Day in and day out one of us would be there with her. Finally after numerous foster homes, my parents finally decided to take them both in. And then Ash came along...And the way he brought the most happiness to her life just to leave her wrecked and begging him for more was beyond me. I couldn't understand. But once again Colt and I took turns when she'd spiral over him as well.

I started to doze off when I was jolted awake with a thought. *Kassidy.* Sloane is playing with fire and doesn't even fucking know it! Every time I try to tell her-something interferes, as if the universe thinks it's hilarious to keep playing this same sick joke.

Lena stirring beside me, dragging me out of my thoughts. I have to get some sleep. I have to make sure I have the energy to handle Sloane when shit hits the fan.

Because when it comes to Sloane and Ash–it most definitely will.

Chapter 41

The morning sunlight poured through the blinds, harsh and intrusive, dragging me awake before my alarm could even ring. My body ached in a way that had nothing to do with sleep – last night's memories of Ash clung to me, heat and tension tangled in my muscles.

I forced myself out of bed, getting dressed in the outfit I had picked out before going to Colt's for dinner last night. No red, no provocations, no reminders of him. Today was AnchorPoint Refuge – my office, my life – my attempt at normalcy after uprooting my entire life for the second time in a row.

The shower was quick, almost mechanical. Hot water rushed over me, but even the steam couldn't wash away the lingering thoughts of Ash's hands, his whispers. I scrubbed harder than necessary, gripping the shower wall as if it could anchor me.

Quinn's note still sat on the counter: *Call me if you need to talk. Don't let him consume you.* I read it twice before shoving it into my bag. She was right, of course. I couldn't let him take over again. Not fully.

Driving to my office, I rehearsed my professional persona in my head – calm, grounded, capable. Trauma therapist. That was my identity now. Helping others survive, helping others reclaim their lives. And maybe, in the process, reminding myself that I could survive too.

AnchorPoint Refuge looked the same as ever – warm lighting, welcoming yet professional, a place that felt like it had been waiting for me. I pushed the door open, inhaling the faint scent of coffee and sanitizer, and took a deep breath.

A familiar voice greeted me. "Sloane! Welcome back." Harper, the office manager, smiled, holding a clipboard. "Let me show you around. We've got some new clients lined up, and some old faces that might be glad to see you home."

"Thanks," I said, forcing a smile. My heart still thudded a little too fast, and not just from nerves.

I walked through the hallways I'd known before – walls lined with inspirational art, soft music playing in the background, therapy rooms that smelled faintly of lavender. It felt like home, but the tension in my chest reminded me that home could still hold chaos.

When I settled into my office, I let myself finally breathe. My desk was neatly arranged, client files stacked and labeled, journals waiting for notes. On the other side of the room, a soft loveseat invited visitors to sink into it, with a beaded beanbag chair tucked into the corner for those who needed space to fidget or decompress. A small table held essential oils and a diffuser that I had pulled from my bag, filling the room with a calming blend of lavender and eucalyptus. Every detail – the muted colors, the soft lighting, the soothing scents – was designed to make this a place of refuge.

I sank into my chair, fingers brushing over the smooth wood, and tried to focus. AnchorPoint wasn't about Ash. It wasn't about Kassidy. It was about me – about the work I loved, the people I helped, and maybe, slowly, the part of me that could survive everything he threw at me.

But even as I set my notepad down and opened my calendar, a shiver ran through me. The pull of him lingered, subtle but persistent, like a shadow at the edge of my vision. I shook my head, forcing it away. Today, I reminded myself, was about the clients, about AnchorPoint, about Sloane – not Ash.

Not today.

By mid-morning, the office had quieted down. The soft hum of the HVAC, faint music in the background, and the occasional shuffle of papers created a rhythm I could almost sink into. I stretched, letting my shoulders relax, and leaned back in my chair.

I grabbed a cup of water from the counter at the far end of the room and walked over to the small window overlooking the street. The city below moved at it's usual pace, people hurrying by, oblivious to my tangled thoughts. I let my gaze drift, focusing on the mundane details – the way sunlight reflected off a car, the flutter of leaves in the breeze –

anything to pull me out of the lingering heat from last night.

Back in my office chair, I straightened a stack of journals, adjusted the diffuser, and ran my fingers over the soft upholstery of the loveseat. It was inviting, calming – almost like the room itself was reminding me that I had control here. For a few moments, I let myself breathe, untangling from the shadows of Ash and the tension Quinn's warning had left me with.

I glanced at the schedule for the rest of the day, briefly thinking of the clients I'd meet. Nothing too specific – just the idea that the work filled the space in my mind and gave me something tangible to hold onto. It was grounding, a reminder that my life wasn't just the chaos he left behind.

I sank back into my chair, letting the quiet hum wrap around me. For now, this was my world. Safe, controlled, mine. And for the first time that morning, I felt the tiniest bit of peace.

By noon, my stomach reminded me I hadn't eaten since my granola bar this morning. I grabbed my bag, slipping on a light jacket, and headed out for a quick lunch. The streets were bustling, but the crisp air and the simple act of walking felt grounding – a brief reprieve from the hum of AnchorPoint.

I walked to a small café just a few blocks away that I use to walk to every day for lunch before I had went to California, and ordered my usual- a caramel latté and croissant, settling into a corner seat, letting the warm sunlight spill across the table. I pulled out my phone to check messages, hoping for a quiet moment to myself.

The vibration made my stomach flip. Ash.

Enough pretending that you don't want me too, damn it! No more games, Sloane. Once and for all, we're fuckin' doing this.

Heat flared in my chest, a mix of irritation and something darker. My fingers hovered over the phone, torn between wanting to reply and knowing I shouldn't. Quinn's warning rang in my head: *Don't let him consume you.*

I shoved the phone back into my bag, pressing my lips together. Today wasn't about him. Not here. Not now. AnchorPoint was my world, and for this small window of time, I had to protect it – and myself.

I picked up my latté and took a slow sip, letting the café's calm hum wrap around me. My mind drifted to nothing in particular – the warmth of the sun, the aroma of coffee, the quiet rhythm of people talking softly around me. For a moment, I let the tension ease, even if just a little.

Even with Ash's text burning in the back of my mind, I reminded myself: I was Sloane. I was in control. And today, I wasn't his.

Chapter 42

The rest of the day passed in a blur of quiet sessions, client check-ins, and organizing schedules. I stayed mostly in the background, letting the work fill my mind and keep Ash at bay. Some sessions were brief, some stretched longer, but each one reminded me why I loved this job – why AnchorPoint Refuge was mine. A place where I could help others reclaim control over their lives.

By late afternoon, the office was emptying. I packed up my things, neatly stacking files and wiping down my desk. The calm of the day contrasted sharply with the fire Ash had left burning in me, but I refused to think about him. Not yet. Today had been about clients, about work, about survival.

As I slid into my car, my phone buzzed. Kassidy's name lit up the screen.

"Hey, babe," she said, voice low and teasing in my ear "Come see me."

Heat pooled low in my stomach. I smiled despite myself. "Yeah... I'll be there soon," I murmured, tossing the phone back into my bag.

She's not Ash and that's why I didn't hesitate.

The ride to her apartment was short, my mind already shifting from work mode to anticipation. But even as I pulled up, a flicker of heat and irritation rose in my chest at the thought of Ash – that damn smirk, those impossible dimples, the way he always knew how to get under my skin. I shoved it down. I wasn't his right now.

The moment I unlocked the door, Kassidy was waiting – eyes dark, grin wicked. Before I could even set my bag down, she grabbed me, pressing her body hard against mine. Her hands were everywhere – cupping, sliding, gripping – and a shiver tore through me.

"I thought you'd never get here," she murmured, voice rough.

Her kiss was fierce, demanding. I tried to push Ash from my mind, but even as her tongue traced mine and her hands moved with possessive precision, he was there – the way he'd touch me, tease me, make me ache and beg. The thought made my pulse spike.

Clothes fell fast. Kassidy's hands never stopped exploring, claiming me with a hunger that left no room for hesitation. She straddled me, grinding hard, teeth grazing my collarbone. I gasped, fingers tangling in her hair. Even as I lost myself to her, my mind flickered to him – that low rumble of his voice, that thrill, that danger.

"I've been waiting for this," Kassidy hissed, teeth scraping my shoulder. "Every second you weren't here, I wanted you more."

Her hands were relentless, pulling me closer until my body arched to meet her. A moan slipped out, unrestrained, and somewhere in the back of my mind I imagined Ash watching, smirking, daring me to forget him. I didn't – not completely – but I let Kassidy take me anyway.

When we finally came together – raw, unrelenting – my body was slick, trembling, heart hammering. Every nerve sang, every ache sharpened, every shadow of him still burning. I collapsed against her, gasping, skin damp and mind a tangle I couldn't untwist.

She rolled to the side, brushing hair from my face, smirk curling her lips. "You're mine tonight."

I laughed breathlessly, because I knew I'd never truly belong to anyone but Ash – but letting myself pretend was enough to keep me sane.

When I finally left her apartment, body still buzzing, mind half-lost in memory, I knew tomorrow would be another day at AnchorPoint. Another day surviving Ash and the chaos he brings.

But tonight had been mine – wild, untamed, a collision of desire and control with his shadow flickering in every stolen breath.

I made my way back to Quinn's and showered. As i was getting ready to lay down, my phone buzzed on the nightstand. I groaned, rolling over and pulling the covers over my head – as if that would hide me from the truth I already knew.

I didn't need to look to know exactly who it was.

Chapter 43

His hand on my throat.
Not soft. Not cruel. Just there — claiming me, pinning me in place.

Ash towers over me, headlights and firelight behind him turning his tattoos blacker, meaner. His grin is lazy, dangerous — the one that always got me in trouble.

I can't move.
I don't want to.

The dream shifts fast. Suddenly I'm on the hood of a car, metal hot under my back, skirt shoved up around my hips. The air is thick with smoke and gasoline, the tang of leather sharp enough to taste. I shiver from more than the heat. My nipples ache under his fingers, my stomach twisting with want. Every nerve is lit, every inch of me humming with memory and need.

He spreads my legs like he has every right to, inked knuckles sliding slow up my inner thighs, teasing, dragging over my slickness. I moan — high, frantic — hips lifting into his touch. My breaths come fast, shallow, mingling with the crackle of flames and the low hum of the city in the dreamscape. I can feel the sweat on my back, hot and sticky, matching the slick heat between my legs.

"You still mine, Sloane?" His voice is a low growl that slides over my skin and into my bones. It vibrates inside me, shakes me to my core.

I should tell him no.
But I don't.

His fingers press into the wet heat between my legs, dragging through me, coating them, spreading me open. I whimper. Arch. Beg without words. I can feel the burn in my thighs from the friction, my core quivering from want, my pulse thrumming violently through my body.

He leans over me, mouth brushing my ear. "Say it."

I choke out something that sounds like please, and then his fingers are inside me — deep, relentless. His thumb stroking my clit, slow and precise at first, then faster, teasing, pushing me closer to the edge. I'm trembling, shaking, thighs quivering, heart hammering. My back arches off the hood, hips driving into his hand, desperate, craving everything. My skin prickles with every brush of his knuckles. Every whisper of his breath sends shivers racing down my spine.

I'm so close I can taste it — heat coiling tight in my belly, every nerve alive, sparking. I grind against his fingers, imagining his weight pressing me down, his mouth bruising my skin, the dangerous heat of him everywhere. My heart pounds, throat tight, and I feel like I could burn alive from the friction of want alone.

"Come on, Sloane. Cum for me." I hear him whisper, dark and cruel and commanding. Every syllable vibrates through me. My skin tingles where his lips might be, every imagined brush of teeth or tongue sending another wave of need through me.

My hips jerk. My toes curl. My thighs shake. The orgasm rips through me like fire, violent and consuming. My back bows hard against the car, a strangled cry tearing from my throat, his name ripped from me in a desperate moan. I can feel the tension spiraling down into my stomach, into my legs, quivering, shaking, trembling in a way that makes me both desperate and dizzy.

And then — just like that — I wake.

I'm throbbing, desperate, soaking. The sheets are twisted and damp. My panties cling wet against me. My clit pulses with an almost painful insistence. Every breath is ragged, every muscle taut and trembling. My back aches from the imaginary weight of him, my thighs sore from grinding, my stomach still curled with want.

I don't even hesitate.

My hand slides between my legs, shoving the soaked fabric aside. Fingers find my swollen flesh — slick, aching — and I rub fast, hard, chasing more of what the dream left me aching for. My other hand claws the sheets, twisting them, trying to ground myself as my body shudders. Every nerve screams for more. Every inch of me craves the weight, the touch, the fire of him.

I picture him – that grin, those black tattoos, the weight of him over me, the way his fingers felt inside me. His voice in my head, low and rough, telling me exactly how he wants me to cum for him. I imagine the heat of his chest against mine, the smell of leather and gasoline, the faint tang of marijuana smoke, the rough press of his knuckles on my thighs, the cruel curl of his lips as he watches me writhe beneath him.

I work myself harder, hips lifting, pressing into my hand, chasing that edge. My fingers dip inside, curl, drag me closer. I bite my lip to keep from crying out, chest heaving, nipples hard and aching, back arching violently with every stroke. My mind fills with him, consuming every corner, leaving no space for anything else.

The orgasm hits like a thunderclap – violent, wet, relentless. My back arches, hips jerking, fingers buried deep as wave after wave rips through me. His name tears from my throat as I convulse, thighs clamping tight, shaking, body left trembling and drenched. I can feel the aftershocks ripple through my legs, through my stomach, through my chest, leaving me gasping and trembling, sated yet raw.

I slump back against the pillows, breath ragged, heart hammering. My thighs are sticky, clit still pulsing, sweat cooling on my skin. The dream clings like smoke. Every corner of the room smells faintly of him – the phantom scent of leather, gasoline, his cologne, curling through my senses and refusing to leave.

I can still hear that dark, low laugh, mocking and satisfied. I imagine the brush of his fingers along my skin, the bite of his thumb against me, the low command in his voice as he tells me what he wants, what I crave, what I'll beg for.

I roll onto my side, clutching the damp sheets, body raw, nerves still buzzing. I hate him. I want him. I ache for him. I know no amount of release – no matter how many times I touch myself, no matter how hard I cum – will ever erase him from my body, from my mind. I want to curse him. I want to push him away. For fuckin' good. But every instinct tells me

I'll fail. He's burned into my skin, my blood, my thoughts.

And deep down, I know he will never be gone.
Not from my dreams.
Not from my body.
Not from my mind.

And yet... even as I try to breathe, even as I clutch the sheets and shiver, I can't deny it. The memory of him, the phantom heat, the ache that coils inside me, the power he holds over me – it's absolute. I ache, I crave, I burn, and I know the hunger for him will never be tamed.

Chapter 44

I roll onto my side, chest heaving, thighs still trembling, sweat cooling across my skin. My fingers curl into the sheets, trying to anchor myself to reality, but the phantom of him still lingers – his hands, his fingers, the ghost of his laugh in my skull.

I pick up my phone, remembering the notification from last night.

I swallow hard. The words feel like a slap:
You think avoiding me will make me go away?

My stomach twists. My body remembers everything – the dream, the ache, the way my fingers had pressed into myself minutes ago in the dark. My breath catches. I press my hand over my mouth, heart racing, pulse thudding in my ears.

I stare at the text, willing it to be some kind of mistake, some prank, anything but him. But it's real.
So real.
Raw.
So poisonous.

I press my lips together, trying to steady the tremor in my hands, trying not to let my body betray me, trying not to think about the way the dream left me quivering, ruined, and aching for him.

I stare at the message too long. My thumb hovers over the reply button, but I don't press it. I can't. I don't even know what I would say.

The silence of Quinn's place presses in, broken only by the faint hum of the city outside. And still – I can feel him. I can feel the memory of his fingers, the press of his body in my mind, the way he had me trembling, gasping, on the edge.

I shake my head, trying to push the thoughts away, but they curl around me like smoke, wrapping me up, sinking into my skin.

Another buzz. Another text.

Ignoring me won't save you, Sloane. You belong to me.

My breath catches in my throat. My fingers dig into the sheets. Heat pools between my legs again, reminding me that my body hasn't forgotten, that my mind hasn't forgotten, that he hasn't left me at all.

I drop the phone onto the bed and curl into myself. My chest heaves. My skin is damp with sweat. My heart is pounding so hard it feels like it will crack my ribs.

I hate him.
I want him.
I can't ever get him out of my head.

The room is silent. But I can hear him.

I can hear the dark, mocking laugh echoing in my mind, curling around me, teasing me, claiming me.

And I know – he's not going anywhere.

I finally shove the phone aside, but the heat in my chest doesn't go away. My body is still on edge, trembling from the dream and the memory of his texts. Every muscle feels tight, wound up, my skin prickling. I need to move, to do something that will make me feel like myself again – or at least like a version of me that can function.

I drag myself out of bed, sticky sheets clinging to my thighs. The bathroom is cold under my bare feet, the tiles shocking against my skin. I stare into the mirror; the reflection staring back at me isn't exactly me. Haunting green-blue eyes, flushed cheeks, lips parted – the ghost of last night's heat still lingering.

I splash water on my face, trying to shake him off, but the memory of the dream claws at me anyway: the feel of his fingers inside me, his thumb circling, that grin, that low, cruel growl.

I brush my teeth mechanically, scrub at my skin, pulling on clothes with trembling hands. Nothing feels right. Every motion is half-mindless autopilot, my thoughts looping back to him, to the text, to the dream, to the ache still pooling low in my stomach.

I grab my bag and phone, already anticipating another message. But for now, nothing. Silence. I tell myself to focus, to pull myself together. AnchorPoint is waiting. Work is waiting. People are waiting. I have to be normal.

The drive is a haze. Music plays from the car stereo, but every note feels like it's bleeding into my skin, reminding me of him, of last night's dream, of the ache that hasn't left.

Every stoplight, every turn, makes my pulse spike. I catch myself gripping the wheel too tight, knuckles white, body tense, legs pressed together instinctively as though trying to hold the heat at bay.

I can't.

And yet I try. AnchorPoint looms ahead, familiar and grounding in its mundane reality. I tell myself to breathe, to slow down, to focus on the work waiting for me – anything but him. But the memory lingers, a phantom brushing my skin, curling in my mind, teasing, reminding me that he's still here.

I park, engine humming softly, and take a long, shaky breath. I stare at the building in front of me, the place I've spent so many days trying to carve out some sense of normalcy. I tell myself I'll walk in like nothing happened, like I'm okay, like I'm not still raw, still craving, still haunted.

I step out of the car, the cold morning air hitting my skin, trying to ground myself. One foot in front of the other. Step after step. I have to be ready. I have to be present. AnchorPoint doesn't care about Ash, or my dreams, or the way my body is still alive with memory his.

But I do.

I step inside, shoulders squared, forcing the normalcy onto my skin like armor. The office smells of coffee and paper and something else that I can't place– and yet, even here, I feel his shadow clinging to me.

Every heartbeat, every glance, every shiver of remembered touch, reminds me he hasn't left.

And I know – no matter how hard I try to ignore him, no matter how much I focus on work, he's already inside me, tangled in my entire being.

I take a deep breath. Today I try my best to forget about Ash Walker.

Chapter 45

AnchorPoint feels too calm today.
Too quiet.

The faint smell of lavender cleaner and brewed coffee hangs in the air, the kind of scent that should settle me, but all it does is make the restless hum under my skin feel louder.

Maybe it's because I barely slept.
Maybe it's because of him.

I grab my phone before I can talk myself out of it, opening the last unread notification – the message from Ash that I'd left there like a splinter.

Ignoring me won't save you, Sloane. You belong to me.

My stomach twists. My thumb hovers over the screen, itching to type something – anything – but I lock the phone and drop it into my bag instead.

No.
Not today.
I'm at work. I'm safe here.

I glance at the clock and force myself to focus. First client of the morning is a new intake – no, a new counseling session with someone they matched me with last night. I pull up the chart, scanning the few notes from the referral. Male. Mid-thirties. History of trauma. Guarded.

Great. My favorite type.

The knock on my office door is soft but firm.

"Come in," I call, standing as the door swings open.

And then I see him.

He's taller than I pictured, all broad shoulders and quiet presence. His hair is dark, a little too long, falling near his brow in a way that makes him look younger – or maybe just untamed. But it's his eyes that catch me – sharp, assessing, like he's already cataloged the whole room before he even steps fully inside.

"You must be Malachai," I say, my voice even though my pulse skips unexpectedly.

He nods once, his expression unreadable.

We shake hands – firm, warm. His palm is calloused, the kind of touch that tells me he's done hard things with those hands, and for some reason, my stomach tightens.

"Have a seat," I say, motioning to the chair across from mine.

He sits, his body language loose but watchful, as if he could bolt at any second if he wanted to.

"How are you feeling about being here today?" I ask gently, settling into my chair and giving him my most open counselor posture.

He studies me for a moment, like he's weighing whether or not I'm worth answering. Then:

"Honestly? Didn't think I'd actually show up."

My lips curve in the faintest smile. "But you did."

He shrugs, one corner of his mouth twitching. "Guess I did."

I start slow, letting him set the pace. He doesn't give me much at first – just clipped answers, short sentences – but he's not shutting down completely either. There's a tension under his voice, a coil wound tight.

Little by little, the edges come off.

He tells me he's been angry lately, not at anyone in particular, just... at everything. He tells me he doesn't sleep much. That he avoids people because they ask too many questions.

"Sounds like you've been carrying a lot by yourself," I say softly.

His gaze snaps to mine. Those eyes are intense – dark enough that it almost feels like a challenge.

"Easier that way," he says finally.

"Easier," I echo, "but not lighter."

Something flickers in his expression – not quite a smile, but something close.

"You make it sound simple," he murmurs.

"It's not." I lean forward slightly, letting the words settle between us. "But you don't have to do it alone anymore. That's why you're here."

He exhales through his nose, not quite a laugh, not quite a sigh. "You don't look like you belong here, you know that?"

The comment catches me off guard. "What does that mean?"

"Most people who do this job..." His eyes drag over my face, my hair, my posture before he finishes. "They're harder. Colder. You don't seem like that."

I let out a quiet breath, almost a laugh. "I get that a lot."

"Not a bad thing." His mouth curves slightly again, deliberate this time.

Something warm flickers in my chest before I push it back down and glance at the clock.

When the hour is up, I stand. "We'll go over a treatment plan next time," I say, keeping my voice steady. "I'll get you scheduled with one of our counselors for weekly sessions."

He stands too, slow and deliberate, and suddenly the space between us feels charged.

"I was hoping I could schedule with you."

My heart gives a traitorous jump, but I keep my face calm. "I have a few openings on my caseload. Let me make sure I can take you on."

That small smile again, sharper this time. "Good. I'd rather talk to you."

The words slide under my skin like a current.

I hand him the paperwork, and his fingers brush mine – not an accident, not this time. My breath catches, just for a second, before I pull my hand back.

"See you next week, Sloane." he says turning to walk out of my office door.

The sound of my name in his voice makes my chest tighten, makes my pulse jump in a way I hate.

When the door clicks shut, I sit back down hard, staring at my desk like it might ground me.

It's just work.
Just a client.

But my body doesn't believe me. My heart is racing, my palms are damp, and all I can think about – infuriatingly – is what Ash would say if he'd seen the way Malachai looked at me just now.

What Ash would do.

The thought makes me shiver.

And that's what scares me most – that for one split second, sitting here in my quiet office, I almost wish he had.

Chapter 46

The morning drags on.

Sessions blur together, clients leaving my office with heavy shoulders and quieter voices than they arrived with. I sit back at my desk between appointments, rubbing my temples, trying to shake the mental fog that Ash left me with. Malachai's quiet intensity still crawls under my skin, but I shove the thought down. Focus. Work. Keep moving.

By noon, I need a break – a real one. I grab my bag and head out the door, making a beeline for the little café just around the corner from AnchorPoint. It's quiet, tucked between a florist and a dry cleaner, the smell of roasted coffee beans and fresh pastries spilling into the street. I push through the door, the little bell jingling overhead, and immediately feel my shoulders relax.

I order my usual – a caramel latté and a croissant – and find a corner table by the window. The quiet hum of the café, the soft clink of cups and spoons, and the warm smell of baked goods make it feel like a tiny bubble separate from the chaos of the morning.

And then my phone rings.

Colt.

Perfect timing. He always knows when I need to talk as I try to shake this morning off.

"Hey!" I say, trying to keep my voice casual.

"Lo! I couldn't wait to tell you!" His excitement bursts through the line, contagious and bright.

I blink. "Uh... okay? What's up?"

"You're gonna be an aunt!"

I freeze mid-sip, my chest skipping a beat. "Wait... what?"

"Elise and I... we're having twins!" His laughter spills through the speaker, full of joy. "I had to tell you first!"

My hand flies to my mouth. "Twins?! Are you serious?!"

"Yes! Two little ones. And you – you're gonna be the best aunt ever."

My stomach flips. My eyes prickle with tears, but I can't stop the grin spreading across my face. "Oh my god, Colt! That's... that's incredible! I'm so happy for you guys!"

"I knew you'd be excited. You've always been my best friend, Lo. You're my other half. I wanted you to hear it first."

I squeal, spinning in my chair, ignoring the curious glance from the barista. "I can't wait! Baby showers! Registries! Themes! Tiny clothes, matching socks! Oh god, Colt, I'm going to plan everything! And I have ideas already – we could do two showers, or one big one with a theme for each baby!"

He laughs, warm and teasing. "You're going to be a whirlwind. But I love it. You'll be involved every step of the way. I promise."

"I can't even! Twins! I'm going to spoil them rotten! And... and name suggestions, and decorations... oh god, I'm losing it!" I laugh so hard my latté nearly tips over.

"You'll be perfect," he says, soft now, almost tender. "And Elise and I will include you in everything."

The call continues with us giggling, brainstorming ridiculous baby shower themes, imagining nursery colors and tiny outfits, and planning how I'll spoil them. My chest feels light, my heart soaring – pure, unfiltered joy.

And then... the call ends.

The phone clicks, and silence crashes down over the café.

The grin falters. My chest tightens, and suddenly the joy feels hollow.

Ash.

I should be floating, riding high on the news, but all I can think about is Ash – the chaos he brings, the way he owns a piece of my heart I can't seem to take back. No baby showers, no twin names, no shared laughter. Just him, distant, untouchable, uncommitted.

I clutch my coffee cup a little tighter, tasting the bitter mix of happiness for Colt and Elise, and sharp longing for something I don't have with Ash.

I take a deep breath, trying to ground myself in the cozy corner of the café, the warm sunlight spilling over the table, the aroma of coffee beans filling my nose. It's okay. I can feel both emotions: joy for my brother, and ache for Ash.

I let the silence settle, sipping the latté slowly, letting the warmth seep into my hands and through my chest. My mind flashes briefly to what life might look like with Ash – a messy, impossible version of this cozy little moment – and I swallow hard.

It hurts.

But I can't let it consume me. I smile faintly, brushing a stray hair behind my ear. The news of twins, the bright spark of family, anchors me, if only for a little while.

I finish my latté, leaving the café with the bell jingling overhead, my pulse still racing, my chest still tight, but carrying a little more light with me as I head back to AnchorPoint. Work awaits, as do my clients, and for now, that's enough to keep me moving forward.

Chapter 47

By the time the last client left, my nerves were shot. I shut the office down on autopilot – diffuser off, light out, door locked. The hallways were quiet as I made my way out, the kind of quiet that almost feels heavy, pressing against you.

Outside, the rain had started – not hard, just enough to slick the pavement and turn the air cold. I pulled my hood up, my bag clutched to my chest.

And then I saw him.

Ash.

Leaning against the hood of my car like he had every right to be there. Like he owned the damn thing. Like he owned me.

My steps faltered. My heart went wild in my chest, hammering so loud I swore it echoed in the empty lot.

He looked up at me from under wet lashes, smirking that slow, dangerous smirk that had always been my undoing. His hoodie was soaked through, dark hair plastered to his forehead, tattoos I could see gleaming slick with rain.

"You're so goddamn stubborn, Sloane."

My throat went dry. "I'm not stubborn." The words came out sharp, but my pulse was thundering, my fingers twitching against my bag strap.

"Stubborn," he said, pushing off my car, closing the space between us, "and in complete fuckin' denial."

I swallowed hard. "About what?"

He stepped right into my space, close enough that the rain

dripping from him hit my skin, close enough that I could smell smoke and leather, and that damn cologne that always drove me wild under the wet asphalt.

"Denial about the fact you want me as bad as I want you."

And then he grabbed my hand.

Heat shot through me like lightning. My breath caught, my heart slamming so hard it hurt.

"I did," I said, voice breaking. "Until Vanessa."

His jaw locked. "Don't," he said, low and sharp.

"You sent me a picture of her in your bed, Ash!" My voice cracked on the words, too loud in the rain-slick parking lot.

His jaw worked. "Yeah, because I was pissed. Because you'd shut me out and I didn't know what else to do to get your attention. But you think she meant a goddamn thing to me? You think anyone else ever does?"

"You think that makes it any fuckin' better? She was still texting you the other night, Ash! Not to mention how you beat Dante so bad he was hospitalized! How the hell am I supposed to look past that? That was uncalled for!"

His eyes went sharp, dangerous. "It wasn't uncalled for."

"Are you kidding me right now?"

"He said he heard you were back in town," Ash said flatly. "He doesn't get to say your name. Not then, not now, not ever. He saw what that got him the first time – and he didn't learn."

"Jesus Christ, Ash." My voice cracked on his name. "You can't just go around beating the shit out of people because they mention me!"

"Watch me." His mouth curved into a grin that didn't reach his eyes.

"You are out of your goddamn mind," I spat, yanking my hand free.

"And you still want me," he fired back instantly, like it was a fact and not up for debate.

"God, you're infuriating!" I threw my hands up, half a scream, half a laugh because he drove me to the damn brink.

He grabbed for my hand again and I yanked it back, chest heaving. "You don't get to do this. You don't get to just—just mind-fuck me whenever you fuckin' feel like it!"

His mouth twisted into that infuriating grin, dimples flashing despite the storm breaking between us. "Why not? You like it when I get in your head."

"You are exasperating!" I threw my hands up again, completely losing my shit.

"And you love it."

The rain was coming down harder now, soaking my hair, running down my face, but I couldn't look away from him. He was every bad decision I'd ever made and the only one I wanted to make again.

When he reached for me again, I stepped back, my breath coming fast and ragged.

"Don't."

For a moment, something almost broke in his face. His voice dropped, quieter now, but no less intense.

"If there's any part of you that can't walk away from us," he said, "meet me tonight. Eight o'clock. Our spot."

My throat tightened.

"And if I don't?"

His jaw worked again. "Then I'm done. No more texts, no more calls, no more games, no more us. You'll never hear from me again. Ill leave you to move on without me in peace. Pick your poison, Sloane."

He turned then, not waiting for my answer. The sound of his boots splashing through puddles echoed as he stalked back to his bike.

The engine roared, thunder rumbling right after like the sky was answering him. And then he was gone – taillight fading red in the rain until there was nothing.

I stood there until I was completely drenched, until my hands were trembling so badly I nearly dropped my keys.

Eight o'clock.

My chest hurt. My pulse wouldn't slow.

I hated him.
I wanted him.
And I didn't know which part of me was going to win.

Chapter 48

By the time I slid behind the wheel, I was soaked, shivering from more than just the rain.

My hair stuck to my face, damp clothes clinging to my skin. The smell of rain and asphalt filled the car as I sat there, chest heaving, heart hammering so loud it almost drowned out the soft squeak of the windshield wipers.

I couldn't move. Couldn't think.

Eight o'clock. Our spot.

His voice was still in my head, low and rough and certain.

The thunder rolled again, shaking the sky, mocking me for sitting here frozen instead of doing what I was supposed to – leaving him in the past.

The whole way through town, my brain wouldn't shut up.

One second, I was furious – gripping the wheel so tight my knuckles turned white, yelling into the empty car, my voice hoarse:

"What the hell is wrong with you, Sloane? He slept with Vanessa. He sent you a picture of her in his bed. He put Dante in the hospital."

My throat ached with it, rage tearing through me like lightning.

The next second, I was breaking apart, throat tight, eyes stinging with tears.

"He said you're it for him. That you always have been. And he looked so... damn it, he looked so sincere."

The rain came harder, pounding the roof like a drumbeat, keeping time with my heart.

I cranked the heat, but I couldn't stop shaking.

"You can't go. You know what happens when you go. He pulls you right back under. You never get to walk away clean."

But the other voice – softer, deadlier – whispered, "You can't not go either. You'll sit here all night staring at the clock, wondering what if. Wondering if this time could've been different."

I clenched my jaw so hard it hurt.

The road blurred through the windshield, the streetlights stretching into glowing streaks. My vision blurred too, and I couldn't tell if it was the storm or my own tears.

"God, I hate you," I muttered, but it sounded like a lie, even to me. My chest ached so hard I wanted to beat on it just to make it stop.

Images slammed into me, sharp as glass:

Ash's hand gripping mine in the rain.
His hoodie soaked through.
The look in his eyes when he said, *you're it for me.*

And then – just as fast – the picture of Vanessa in his bed. Her hair splayed across his pillow. That smug little smile like she'd won, like she had something that belonged to me. *Because she fuckin' did.*

My stomach twisted until I felt nauseous.

I fumbled with the radio, desperate for something to drown him out, but of course the universe was cruel. The song that came on was one of ours. The one that had been playing from his Harley when he kissed me at Colt's football practice, his hand cupping my jaw like I was something precious. Like I meant something to him.

The flashback hit so hard I had to gasp for air.

I slammed the button to skip, but it was too late – the dam had broken, and the memories poured in fast, merciless:

Ash grinning at me through the smoke of a bonfire.
His voice, low and teasing, saying my name like a secret.
His fingers tangled in my hair, pulling just enough to make my knees weak.
The night he called me from jail and made me—

I shook my head so hard it made me dizzy, swearing under my breath.

"No. We're not doing this. Not tonight." I told myself.

But my pulse didn't get the memo.

By the time I pulled into Quinn's driveway, I was half ready to turn around and head straight to the field – and half ready to drive until I ran out of gas just to keep myself from doing exactly that.

I sat in the car, rain hammering the windshield like it wanted in, breath coming too fast.

Quinn's house was inviting, warm, and safe. For one fragile second, I imagined going inside, letting her take one look at me and know, letting her make me tea, crawl into bed, pretend this entire night never happened.

But my brain wouldn't stop whispering.

Eight o'clock. Eight o'clock. Eight o'clock.

I grabbed my phone off the passenger seat, staring at the black screen until it lit up with my own reflection.

6:17.

My stomach dropped.

An hour and forty-three minutes.

I could sit here.

I could go inside and lock the door and prove to myself that I was finally done.

Or I could get back in the car and drive to him, knowing exactly what would happen if I did.

My heart slammed against my ribs, frantic.

Would he be there, waiting with open arms?

Would he be angry if I didn't show up?

Would he look at me the way he did in the parking lot – like I was the only thing in the world he wanted?

Would he touch me again like I was the only thing that ever made sense to him?

My chest felt tight, too tight, like there wasn't enough air in the car.

I dropped my forehead to the steering wheel, tears hot now, mixing with the rain on my face.

"I can't do this anymore," I whispered, but my voice cracked on the word can't.

I sat there like that until my breathing slowed, until the thunder quieted into low, distant rumbles.

But still, my brain wouldn't stop chanting, my pulse wouldn't stop racing, my body wouldn't stop humming with the need to see him – just one more time.

I closed my eyes and let the storm rage outside while I tried to decide which part of me was going to win – the part that wanted to save myself, or the part that still wanted him enough to drown myself and not care about the consequences.

Chapter 49

Quinn was in the kitchen when I came in, rain still dripping off me, hair plastered to my face.

She took one look at me and frowned. "Lo... what happened?"

I didn't answer right away. My bag slid off my shoulder and hit the floor with a thud. I leaned against the counter, heart still trying to punch it's way out of my chest.

"Ash happened," I said finally, voice flat.

Quinn's eyebrows shot up. "What do you mean Ash happened?"

I pressed my palms to the edge of the counter, like holding onto something solid might keep me from flying apart. "He was at AnchorPoint. Waiting for me in the parking lot."

Her face darkened. "What did he say?"

I swallowed hard. The words felt heavy in my mouth. "He told me to stop being stubborn. That I want him as bad as he wants me."

Quinn made a face. "Typical Ash Walker bullshit."

"Yeah, well," I said, my throat thick, "then he told me to meet him at the football field at eight. Said if I didn't show, he's done. For good."

The kitchen went quiet. Only the hum of the refrigerator and the faint patter of rain filled the air.

Quinn leaned back against the counter opposite me, crossing her arms. "And what are you gonna do?"

"I don't know," I admitted, my voice cracking more than I wanted it to. "Part of me wants to lock myself in this house and throw my phone in the damn river so I can't even think about going. And part of me—" I broke off, staring at the floor, heart hammering. "Part of me wants to get in the car and never hit the brakes until I'm there."

Quinn's expression softened and she was quiet for a long moment, studying me. "Sloane... you don't owe him anything. Not after Vanessa. Not after Dante."

My throat closed. "I know."

"Do you?" she pressed gently. "Because I'm not sure you do. That guy nearly killed Dante. He—"

"It wasn't uncalled for," I cut in, the words slipping out before I could stop them.

Quinn blinked. "Excuse me?"

I swallowed hard, heart thudding. "That's what he said. Dante shouldn't have been running his mouth, saying he heard I was back in town. He'd already seen what that got him once before. He didn't learn. And Ash—he made sure he did this time, I guess."

The room went quiet except for the sound of the rain against the windows. Quinn just stared at me, her expression unreadable.

"And that sounds okay to you?" she asked finally, voice sharp with disbelief.

I flinched. "No. God, no. But a part of me understands it, and that scares me. It scares me how much I—"

"How much you still love him," she finished for me.

I closed my eyes. "Yeah."

I scrubbed my hands over my face, like that could wipe him off me. "I can't keep doing this. I either have to go and get it out of my system, or I have to let him go for good."

Silence stretched between us, heavy.

Finally, Quinn asked gently, "What about Kassidy?"

My chest tightened. Kassidy. Sweet, patient Kassidy who had been there when I was falling apart.

"If I go," I said, voice low, "I'm done with her. I can't keep stringing her along while I'm this—" I gestured at myself, at the shaking hands, the wild eyes. "While I'm this messed up over him."

Quinn looked like she wanted to argue but she didn't. She just nodded once, slow, like she understood and hated it at the same time.

I turned to leave, but then stopped, hand on the doorway as Quinn said "There's something I need to tell you about Kass—"

And then, because the universe is cruel, Lena's voice rang out from the front of the house.

"Hey! Anyone home?"

I cursed under my breath. Quinn gave me an apologetic look.

"We'll talk later," I muttered, grabbing my bag and heading toward the stairs before Lena could corner me.

In my room, I stripped out of my damp clothes, tossing them in a pile, and stood in front of the mirror. My reflection looked wrecked – hair a mess, mascara smudged, cheeks flushed.

I should stay. I should climb into bed, turn my phone off, let Quinn and Lena distract me until the clock runs out.

Instead, I found myself pulling on jeans, a black hoodie, sneakers. My hands shook as I zipped up the hoodie, like my body already knew what decision I was about to make.

When I came back downstairs, Lena was in the kitchen talking to Quinn. She looked up at me, smiling like nothing was wrong.

"Going out?" Lena asked.

I nodded once, too fast. "Yeah. Just need some air."

Quinn's eyes met mine across the room. She didn't say anything, but I saw the understanding there, the warning too.

My heart pounded as I grabbed my keys and slipped out into the rain again.

By the time I slid behind the wheel, my pulse was a roar in my ears.

This was it. No more back and forth.

The storm had slowed to a steady drizzle, the sky a dark, heavy gray. I put the car in gear and backed out, tires crunching on wet gravel, and told myself I was just going for a drive.

But my hands didn't turn toward anywhere safe.

They turned toward the field.

The closer I got, the faster my heart raced. My stomach twisted so tight I could barely breathe.

The whole way there, I kept whispering to myself, "This is it. This is it."

Either I'd find him there and let him pull me back under...

Or I'd stand in the rain and tell him no for the last time.

Either way, something was ending tonight.

Chapter 50

The rain had slowed to a mist by the time I had finally backed out of Quinn's driveway, but everything still looked wet, shining like glass. It felt like the whole town had been rinsed clean, except for me. I was a mess – pulse hammering, stomach twisting, knuckles white around the steering wheel as I pulled onto the road.

The wipers made lazy swipes, just enough to smear the mist across the glass and make the world look blurry and unreal. Too quiet. Too calm. Like the whole night was holding its breath, waiting to see if I would actually do the thing I swore I wouldn't do.

But I kept driving anyway.

The tires hissed over the wet pavement, carrying me toward the edge of town, toward him, toward the thing I'd been running from for years.

My chest ached, too tight, like there wasn't enough air in the car. I turned the heat up anyway, but I couldn't stop shivering. The vents blew warm air against my face, but my bones still felt cold – maybe from the rain, maybe from what I was about to do.

And then the memories started.

Not random flashes, not disjointed pieces – but moments that pulled together into a timeline of him, of us, of everything I couldn't quit.

The summer I snuck out to meet him behind the old high school gym. He was waiting, leaning against his car, grinning like he knew exactly what he did to me. That laugh – low and rough – it rolled through the night air and made my stomach flip. I remembered the way his hands rested on my hips, sure and claiming, grounding me in ways I shouldn't have let him.

Then the night he came to my window after one of my worst fights with Colt I had ever had...It was about Ash but I didn't let him know that.

We sat on the roof, passing a blunt back and forth under the stars, shoulders brushing. His voice was soft, teasing, coaxing me to stop being so hard on myself – to let someone in. Even then, I had sworn I'd resist, but his closeness made it impossible.

I gritted my teeth and pressed harder on the accelerator, like maybe I could outrun the ache. But the memories kept coming.

The first time he touched my tattoo. His thumb traced the curve along my ribs, making me shiver in a way I'd never admit to anyone else.

And then the darker pieces. The times he pushed too far. Ember. Dante. Vanessa. The picture of her lying in his bed, the smug little smirk like she'd won something I wasn't supposed to care about, all of it spiraling together. My stomach tightened into knots. My hands ached on the wheel.

"You should turn around. You should just go home," I whispered to myself. But my foot stayed on the gas.

Because underneath all of it – the hurt, the anger, the betrayal – there was something else. Something raw and aching and impossible to ignore.

His voice looped in my head, quiet but insistent: *You're it for me, Sloane. You always have been.*

And I believed him.

God help me, I believed him.

The drizzle thinned even more until it was barely there, just a faint mist hanging in the air, turning the world silver under the streetlights.

The road curved toward the edge of town, and my stomach twisted tighter with every turn. My pulse was everywhere – in my neck, in my wrists, in my teeth – until it felt like my whole body was just one loud, thudding heartbeat.

I could still turn around.

I could still save myself.

But I didn't.

I kept going.

Because I wasn't ready to let him go.

Not yet.

The memories now came fast, jagged, looping into one another.

That night at the gas station parking lot – he had cornered me, eyes dark, smirk teasing, like he knew I had nowhere to run. The way he kissed me with so much intensity, my legs buckled and he had to hold me upright, smirking about how he makes my knees weak.

The bonfire that summer when he kissed me under the stars, and I thought I could forget him the next day – and I failed miserably.

The time he held me after the voicemail I left Colt, murmuring things I can't even remember now, just the weight of his presence, steady and relentless.

The way he'd said my name in the dark, like it belonged to him alone, and my chest had clenched in both fear and want and a hunger for the fire he lit in me.

And then the bloody video of Dante beaten half to death flashed through. Beaten, furious and humiliated, and Ash saying it wasn't uncalled for – that the warning was necessary, that he couldn't let him forget what happened the first time. My jaw tightened. How could I even look past that? How could I let it slide and still want him?

But I did.

The memories made the car feel smaller, hotter, the mist pressing against the windows like the night was trying to close in on me. My stomach twisted so tight I thought I might throw up. My heart thudded, my teeth felt brittle, my pulse ringing in my ears.

Vanessa's face pushed into my head again, and this time it felt like a dare. Like she was still smirking at me from his bed, still taunting me.

"Not this time," I muttered to myself, gripping the wheel tighter, pressing harder on the gas.

Finally, the familiar side street appeared up ahead, the narrow one that led to the football field.

I slowed, breath catching like I'd just run a mile.

The alleyway stretched dark and wet before me, puddles glinting under the lone flickering streetlight like little warning signs. Each one looked like a mark – a don't do it, walk away, save yourself – but I couldn't.

My hands tightened on the wheel until my palms ached.

This was it.

If I turned in, there was no taking it back.

I eased the car into the turn anyway, heart hammering so loud it felt like it filled the whole car.

And for the first time since I left Quinn's driveway, I let myself believe I wasn't going to turn around.

Chapter 51

"I knew you'd come," Ash said cockily, leaning back on his hands against the damp blanket, hair plastered to his forehead from the mist.

"Don't go getting a big head," I replied, trying to keep my voice calm even though my pulse was hammering.

He smirked, dimples flashing, that magnetic pull making my stomach twist. "Oh, I already have one. You just keep feeding it."

The blanket was spread over the wet grass, a bottle of bourbon sitting between us, a blunt rolled and ready, and a small Bluetooth speaker quietly filling the night with lazy music.

I sank down across from him, letting the tension of months of running slip from my shoulders. He poured the bourbon slowly, deliberately, his hand brushing mine as he handed me a glass. My fingers tingled at the contact.

"So..." he said, eyes catching the glow of the speaker lights, "how's life been while you've been avoiding me?"

I laughed softly, thinking to myself, *pure fucking hell. Life without you is pure hell.* But out loud I said, "Keeping people alive. Making sure they don't unravel... shit like that. You know, saving the world one fucked-up trauma case at a time."

He chuckled low, shaking his head. "And here I thought you'd been missing me."

"I—" I faltered, swallowing against the tightness in my throat. "Maybe I have."

His grin widened, cocky and infuriating. "Maybe you have. But you're still pretending you don't."

I rolled my eyes but couldn't stop the small laugh that escaped me. “You’re insufferable.”

“And you wouldn't want it any other way” he countered instantly.

We drank. We laughed. The blunt made the air thick and sweet, the music softening the night until it folded around us like a haze. We argued playfully over memories – the summer night he caught me sneaking out after I’d told him I loved him in the abandoned building, my mud-stained shoes, the rooftop smoke sessions with Colt nowhere near approving, the time he threw me into a dumpster just to see me yell at him because he thinks it's "Sexy when I'm pissed." Each memory made me ache, made me want him, made me hate myself for still needing him so damn badly.

“You remember the time you tried to steal my hoodie and ended up tripping over the porch step?” he asked, smirk tugging at his lips.

“I remember because you laughed so hard you almost fell into the fire pit,” I shot back, shaking my head.

He grinned, low and cocky. “Exactly. I was worried you’d break your pretty little ankle. But you didn’t. You got lucky.”

I smirked, nudging him lightly. “Careful. Compliments from you come with a price.”

“And you love paying it,” he whispered, eyes darkening, smoldering.

The night stretched lazily around us. We talked, we reminisced, we flirted and argued, letting our guards down in ways neither of us had in years. I let myself relax – just for a little while – into the walking chaos that was Ash Walker.

Then he got quiet. That rare, sudden stillness that made my chest tighten.

“Why’d you leave me, Sloane?” he asked, voice low, edged with a pain I hadn’t let myself see until now. “Why’d you wait until I finally confessed what you do to me just to run out of my life?”

I froze, my chest twisting. His eyes – the raw vulnerability in them – broke something open inside me.

"Ash..." I murmured, my hand finding his arm, warm and grounding. "I'm sorry. I didn't realize at the time how much damage it would cause– to both of us. I was scared. Hearing you say those things that night... I had only ever imagined it. And when you really said them... I felt like it was just another game. Because, let's be real, Ash, it's always a game with us–somehow, some way."

His voice softened but stayed firm. "I wouldn't have told you those things, Sloane, if it was a game. I meant that shit."

My chest ached, tears pricking my eyes. "Every part of me screamed to run, so I listened. I'm sorry I wasn't brave enough to save us."

"You don't have to be brave tonight. Not with me, just accept what this is, my love." he said, his thumb brushing over the back of my hand – deliberate, lingering.

Heat curled low in my belly, my pulse hammering so loud I felt it in my ears. I leaned toward him. He mirrored me, eyes dark, magnetic. And then our lips met.

Soft at first, tentative, testing boundaries we had both danced around for months. But the kiss deepened quickly – fierce, consuming. My hands tangled in his damp hair as his traced the curve of my spine, pulling me closer, closer, until there was no space left between us. The bourbon warmth, the blunt haze, the soft music, the cool night air – it all vanished. There was only this: him, me, and the fire that always burned when we got too close.

We broke apart just long enough to gasp for breath, laugh softly, and then he pulled me back in, teeth grazing my bottom lip, smirk pressed against my mouth. The tension between us ignited, wrapping itself around every nerve ending until I was shaking.

"About time," he murmured, voice low, teasing, cocky.

"You're impossible," I panted, chest rising and falling.

"Yep – and that's why you can't get enough of me," he whispered against my lips, dimples flashing.

I laughed softly, breathless, and let myself fall into it – into him. Every argument, every betrayal, every fight – none of it mattered right now. There was only this: Ash, me, and the chaotic, reckless love we couldn't untangle.

His lips brushed along my jaw, then lower to my neck, and I shivered at the heat of him, the intoxicating chaos that followed him like a shadow.

"You know," he whispered, hands gripping my hips, pulling me flush against him, "I've missed this. Missed you. Missed... us."

"I know," I breathed, shivering against him. "Me too."

We kissed again – hot, urgent, magnetic – until the night folded around us completely. Every laugh, every argument, every memory had led to this moment.

Finally, I pulled back, forehead pressed to his, breath uneven. "Every part of me is screaming for me to run again, Ash." My voice trembled as I shook against him.

His voice was calm, certain. "Yeah? Well, I'll be waiting to stop you. I'm not letting you go this time."

I laughed breathlessly, the sound breaking, surrendering to it fully. The bourbon had warmed us, the blunt had softened the edges, and the night – chaotic, calm, magnetic – held us in a way the rest of the world never could.

I kissed his cheek, tasting the faint tang of smoke and bourbon. "Are we really doing this, Ash? Are we finally going to embrace this impossible love we've got?"

"Damn straight we are, my love," he said, pulling me in, heat and chaos coiling tight around us, magnetic and consuming. "There's no other way. When we're apart, we crave each other. We fiend for each other. This is the only thing that's ever made sense for us, Sloane. We've got to embrace it – stop running from it."

His grin flashed again as he wrapped me tighter in his arms.

We stayed like that, tangled together on the damp blanket, the misty night around us, the music a soft soundtrack to our laughter, kisses, and whispered confessions. There was no past, no future, no what-ifs.

There was only this – chaotic, reckless, hot, undeniable.

And for the first time in years, I let myself believe it could actually work.

Chapter 52

I barely had time to catch my breath before Ash pressed back against me, lips claiming mine with a hunger that had been coiled tight for years, tongue ring skidding in my mouth, his hands everywhere – touching, gripping, memorizing. Every inch of him was a brand on my skin, every press of mouth and body igniting fire along every nerve ending.

He lifted my hips, pressing, shifting, and I gasped again, grinding against him without thinking.

"Ash... fuck..." I moaned his name, the sound ripped raw and desperate from somewhere deep in my chest.

His fingers slid under my shirt, tracing the curve of my waist, curling over my ribs, teasing, pressing until my back arched. My lips brushed his jaw, teeth grazing, tasting him, feeling the shiver ripple through him under my touch.

Twenty years. Twenty long, aching years of wanting him, hating him, craving him – all of it burned away with the first press of his mouth to mine, the first hard, claiming thrust of his hips, the first hoarse moan that tore from my throat.

I tangled my hands in his damp hair, dragging him closer, and he groaned, a low, guttural sound as his body pressed against mine – hot, solid, unrelenting.

"God, Sloane..." he breathed, voice thick, rough, urgent against my ear, teeth grazing the shell and pulling a sound out of me I didn't know I could make. "I've fucking wanted this..."

And I had to. For damn near two decades. Finally, we were giving in, after all this time.

I gasped, hips tilting, grinding back against him, every thrum of want between us winding tighter, spreading low and hot, curling through my chest and around my ribs, setting me on fire.

His hands moved with precision — teasing, gripping, claiming — sliding over slick skin, under clothes, over curves, dragging moans out of me I'd been holding in for years. His mouth devoured mine, teeth grazing, tongue sliding, hot and demanding, his voice rough and sinful as he murmured my name, making my whole body shiver.

I pressed harder into him, voice breaking, trembling. "Ash... please... oh fuck..."

He groaned, low and guttural, grinding harder against me, every thrust and shift claiming, insisting, setting me alight.

I let him tip me back onto the damp blanket, fingers still tangled in his hair, nails dragging down his back, pulling him closer, closer, until there was no space left. His hips pinned me, hard and relentless, hands clutching my skin, dragging me higher, deeper, into the fire I'd been running from for years.

"Fuck... Sloane..." he rasped, teeth grazing my collarbone, thumb circling, teasing, pressing until I cried out. "You're mine. Forever."

"Yes... yes... mine too... oh fuck, Ash..." My voice cracked as my hips rocked up to meet him, desperate, shaking, my lips pressed to his shoulder, teeth grazing, my body breaking open around his name.

He gripped my hips, pulling me into each deep, unrelenting thrust, forcing every moan, every gasp out of me until my chest arched and my body couldn't take it anymore.

"Don't stop," I begged, nails clawing at his back, clinging, pressing myself flush to him, heat coiling so tight I thought I might shatter.

He kissed me hard, teeth grazing, tongue sliding, moans swallowed between us, the night spinning away until there was nothing but heat, breath, and the pounding of our hearts.

His thrusts turned rougher, deeper, dragging me closer and closer until I was trembling so hard my legs threatened to give out beneath me.

We moved together – wild, relentless, bodies slick and shaking, gasping each other's names, voices raw, desperate, echoing in the misty night. Twenty years of restraint, of waiting, of craving – all of it erupted into this: chaos, fire, need.

He rolled us, pressing me into the blanket, his chest slick against mine, lips claiming, teeth nipping, hands gripping everywhere at once. I wrapped my legs around him, nails digging into his shoulders, moaning his name again and again until my throat went raw, until the world narrowed down to this unbearable, perfect heat.

"Fuck, Sloane... you're mine. So fucking tight..." he growled, each thrust harder, rougher, breaking me open, his voice equal parts feral and worshipful.

Two whole decades of lust, desire, want, and need wrapped up into this very moment right here.

I arched under him, pressed, rocked, shivered, every muscle tensing as heat and want crashed through me.

We were a tangle of limbs, teeth, lips, sweat, and desperation – each movement a confession, each kiss an apology, each thrust a promise.

And then the wave hit me. Hard. Low and consuming, ripping through every nerve ending, leaving me gasping and shuddering, clutching him with everything I had, crying his name like it could hold me together.

He didn't stop – not until his own release tore through him, his body locking tight against mine, voice ragged, teeth grazing my shoulder as he groaned my name, claiming me even as he shuddered against me.

We collapsed together, chest to chest, bodies trembling and slick, the night air cool on sweat-damp skin. Our hearts pounded in sync, breaths ragged, his hands holding me tight against him like he never wanted to let go.

I buried my face against his chest, inhaling the scent of sweat, bourbon, smoke, him – magnetic, impossible.

"I'm never letting you go," he murmured, voice low and rough, teeth grazing my shoulder, his grip possessive, grounding me in a way that made me shiver all over again.

"Never," I whispered back, voice shaking as I clung to him, letting his name slip from my lips like a prayer.

"Five years since I've felt your arms around me" I breathed, unable to stop the tremor in my chest.

"Yeah," he said, brushing his lips against mine, eyes dark and smoldering, as he pulled me closer. "Every damn second was worth the wait."

For once, I didn't fight it. Didn't argue. Didn't run. I just stayed there – tangled with him in the damp night, my body still buzzing, my pulse still screaming, finally letting go of everything but us.

For two decades, we had waited, fought, run, and come back again. And now, here, on that blanket, on that wet ground, in the mist, we finally stopped running. We finally accepted the inevitable.

No past. No future. No games. No hesitation.

Only fire. Only chaos. Only the magnetic, undeniable pull of us.

And for the first time in years – maybe ever – I let myself fall completely. In every way.

All. Damn. Night. Long.

Chapter 53

The first golden rays of morning filtered over the football field, spilling across the worn turf and warming our tangled limbs. I blinked awake, still caught in the haze of sleep, my body pressed against Ash's in a way that made my heart both ache and race. The night hadn't ended; it had just paused. Every muscle, every nerve in me still remembered him – the heat of his skin, the press of his lips, the way our bodies fit together like they had always known how.

"It really wasn't a dream," I whispered, my voice barely carrying over the faint rustle of the morning breeze. My fingers brushed against his chest, tracing the familiar curve of muscle, and I couldn't help but let my eyes linger on him. This was the first time I'd been close enough without running to really take in all his skin covered in ink.

A barbed wire circled the base of his neck, tight and sharp, a warning etched in ink that framed the chaos below. Across his chest, a busted, crumbling heart burned in dark flames, wrapped in jagged chains, the black-and-gray ink twisting with muscle and shadow – dangerous, raw, alive.

His right arm spiraled with the Milky Way, stars and constellations hidden within the swirling galaxy, and somewhere in the starlight I swear I could see my name subtly etched, hidden but unmistakable. Toward his hand, the cosmic chaos fractured into jagged streaks, comets and starlight twisting into claw-like shapes that seemed ready to rip or ignite with a single movement.

On his left arm, a half-sleeve of dark thorns, shattered skulls, and twisting flames curled down his bicep, a testament to destruction and raw power. On his forearm, an apple with a bite taken out of it, wrapped in a sinuous serpent, coiled like it could strike at any moment – both a warning and a temptation.

Even his left ribcage carried fire and rebirth – a phoenix rising from ashes, wings outstretched, feathers sharp and jagged, flames licking upward, the ink alive with motion. Every inch of him screamed danger, chaos, and obsession, tethering me to him in ways I couldn't — and wouldn't — escape.

"No, babe. It wasn't. We really happened," Ash murmured, his hand cupping my face as he pulled me closer. His lips found mine again, slow and claiming, soft but full of a hunger that had been coiled tight for years. A shiver ran through me, and my breath caught in my throat as our bodies pressed together, skin against skin, each touch igniting every nerve ending like wildfire.

"So... what does this mean for us now?" I asked, my voice small but full of hope, a tremor betraying the nervous excitement I couldn't contain. I tilted my head up to meet his eyes, searching for some sign that he felt the same way — that what had happened wasn't just an accident, a fleeting thing doomed to vanish with the morning light.

Ash's lips curved in a smile that made my stomach twist and melt all at once. He kissed me again, lingering, his thumb brushing against my jawline, and for a heartbeat, the world felt quiet, perfect, as though it had folded around us.

Then my phone buzzed beside me. Cage's name flashed across the screen, bright and insistent, breaking the fragile calm. I froze, my pulse spiking, confusion knotting in my stomach.

Ash's head shot up, his eyes darkening almost instantly, the air around him shifting from warm intimacy to charged electricity. "And you say I'm the one playing games, Sloane! You're still talking to your fucking ex—the man you were going to marry!" His voice cracked sharp, and suddenly every inch of calm I'd felt evaporated.

I flinched at his accusation, my hands trembling slightly as I fumbled for my phone. "Ash, I'm not! And fuck you for making me feel guilty for trying to move on from you! Maybe you should have done the fucking same!" I yelled, frustration and hurt colliding in a storm I hadn't meant to summon. My voice carried across the empty field, rough and raw, trembling with disbelief.

"You don't think I didn't fuckin' try?!" His voice rose, shaking with anger and heartbreak, every word hitting me like a hammer. "I even gave the bitch my last name!"

I froze, mouth falling open, my chest tightening so hard I thought I might choke. Pain hit like a freight train, nausea twisting my stomach. My fingers clutched at the grass beneath me as my brain scrambled to process the words. "You... what?" I whispered, voice shaking, disbelief blazing in my eyes.

Ash ran a hand over his face, pacing the field, the sunlight catching the sharp lines of his jaw, highlighting the tension in every muscle. "Yeah. I... married her. Gave her my last name. I didn't know how to survive you leaving, Sloane."

The world shifted beneath me. My phone buzzed again, Cage's name blinking mockingly, a cruel reminder that the past had not released it's grip on us. I stumbled back slightly, pressing my hands against my knees as my chest heaved. "You... married someone? While... while I–"

"It's not like that was the plan, Sloane! I was trying to forget you! Maybe you should've actually done the same instead of coming back for me!" His voice broke, carrying a mix of fury, regret, and raw heartbreak. He ran both hands through his hair, pacing again, the sun painting him in gold and shadow, every step echoing the chaos in his chest.

I dropped to the grass beside him, feeling my knees go weak, the heat of the morning sun now harsh on my skin. "I... I can't believe you," I whispered, my hands shaking as I reached for him, needing him and hating him at the same time. "After everything... after us..."

The sun cut through the field, harsh and unyielding, and my phone buzzed again. Cage's name blinked at me like a warning, as Ash pulled his arm out of my reach, seeing it too. I swallowed hard, tears stinging, every nerve screaming betrayal and heartbreak.

"Sloane, she was nothing," Ash said again, desperate.

I looked at him, and all I could see was what we had lost. I wanted to hate him, to scream, to run, but my body refused.

"I... I can't do this," I whispered, voice breaking.

He didn't answer. He just stared back, fury and guilt and desperation etched into every line of his face. The space between us was heavy, and I realized, with a gut punch that left me hollow, that nothing – not love, not lust, not even our tangled nights – could erase what had been done.

And in that silence, with the phone still buzzing, the betrayal laid bare, I understood: I could love him. I could hate him. But either way, I'd never survive the pull of Ash Walker.

Epilogue

He said it like it wasn't going to wreck me. Like it wasn't about to split me wide the fuck open.

I gave her my last name.

God, even the echo of his words burned.

My fingers went numb. The grass beneath me felt unreal—just color and texture without meaning. I could still smell him on my skin, taste him in the back of my throat, feel the ghost of his hands on my body. And suddenly it all felt dirty. Every breath, every touch, every I missed you.

The phone buzzed again, Cage's name flashing across the screen like the world's cruelest joke.

I stood back up, disoriented, disassociation coming on strong.

I turned away from him. I didn't know why—instinct maybe, or survival. My body just moved, trying to find air that wasn't laced with him.

Ash's voice broke behind me, words crashing into each other. "It wasn't like that, Sloane! Please! I was trying to forget you. You left me—what the hell was I supposed to do? Please baby—don't walk away—not when we are so goddamn close!"

He was pleading and I didn't give a shit. I couldn't hear him anymore. My pulse drowned everything out. My heart was pounding so loud it blurred into a roar in my ears.

My knees didn't buckle. I didn't scream. I forgot to even breathe.

The world just... stopped.

The golden light of the morning sun felt harsh, too bright, illuminating the man that was just standing in front of me who had just become a stranger. *Married.* The word was a physical thing, a shard of glass stuck in my throat.

The wind caught my hair, but I didn't feel it. My body wasn't here anymore. My mind was back on that blanket years ago, his lips on mine, his voice whispering things he had no right to whisper. My body had been his altar, his confession booth, his goddamn salvation.

And now—he was *married.*

I was in my car. I didn't remember walking to it. My hand was on the key, but it was shaking so hard it took at least three tries to get it into the ignition. The engine roared to life, and I slammed the car into reverse, gravel spitting from under the tires.

I drove. I didn't know where. I just pressed my foot to the gas, "running" from him and the heartbreak he hits me with every time I think we stand a chance, just like he always fucking did.

But this—*this*— was different. He gave someone that wasn't me his last name. He made someone that wasn't me—his goddamn *wife.*

The jealousy, the envy, the betrayal, the pain in my chest I couldn't shake no matter how much I tried. It was all too much. I couldn't breathe. Like the car was closing in on me, suffocating me, caving my chest in.

And I was begging for it to. I was begging for something—anything to take me right the fuck out so I didn't have to feel this unrelenting ache in my entire being.

The road blurred into nothing. My reflection in the rearview mirror was pale, hollow, and foreign. The hum of the engine was the only sound in the world. My heartbeat didn't even feel like my own anymore.

Ten minutes passed—or maybe an hour. I don't really know how long. Time had no shape.

Then the numbness cracked.

"Married."

The whisper came out like a curse, soft but venomous.

And that's when it hit me.

The pain of knowing I'll never have the love I want so bad with Ash Walker.

Not the delicate, aching kind that comes with heartbreak. No, this was violent. This was bone-deep, primal rage that clawed its way out of me with bloodied fingers and refused to be swallowed back down.

I walked away from Cage for *this.* He let me burn my one safe, stable life to the fucking ground, all while he was *married!*

He held me.
He kissed me.
He wrecked me all night fucking long... and the whole time—*married.*

Who? Who the fuck did he marry? Who the fuck is it that gets to call him her *husband?!?!*

I slammed my fists against the steering wheel, once, twice, three times, the impact vibrating up my arms.

Tears blurred my vision, hot and furious, and I couldn't see the road anymore. I swerved onto the gravel shoulder of a two-lane road, the car skidding to a stop in a cloud of dust.

My stomach turned, knots multiplying, making me sick. I opened my car door and started throwing up on the side of the road.

You son of a bitch!" I spat, wiping my mouth. The sound ripping out of me, raw and animalistic.

I was hyperventilating, choking on sobs that felt like they were tearing me apart from the inside. I was furious at him, but I was disgusted with myself. I was a fool. An idiot.

The addict who always came back, begging for another hit, only to find out the poison was laced with something even deadlier. The addict that thought maybe this time the drug wouldn't kill her.

I closed my door and took a drink of my water in the cup holder.

I needed it to stop. All of it. The pain. The memories. The spiral. The goddamn betrayal.

My hands trembled as I ripped my bag open, fumbling for the Backwoods I'd rolled. I lit it, the cherry flaring bright in the dim car, and took a deep, desperate drag. The smoke filled my lungs, but it didn't work. It couldn't touch this. I took another deep breath of it anyways.

I needed more. I needed numb. I needed *wreckage*.

I threw the car back in gear and drove to the first gas station I saw. The fluorescent lights felt too bright, the cashier's bored "hello" like an insult. I grabbed the first bottle of whiskey I saw on the shelf—cheap, harsh, perfect.

Back in the car, I tore the seal off and took a long, burning pull. The whiskey was fire, scalding a path down my throat, and I welcomed it. I took another, choking as it hit my empty stomach.

I sat there, the open bottle on the passenger seat, the blunt smoldering in the ashtray. The rage was gone, replaced by that terrifying, hollow emptiness.

The dissociation was back, but this time it was heavy, suffocating. I didn't know anything anymore.

I needed an anchor before I completely drowned myself in him and the memories I needed to bury. I needed to forget.

I couldn't call Colt. I couldn't bear the shame, the look in his eyes, the "I told you so" he would be too kind to say but would be thinking anyway. He had warned me. I couldn't stand the thought of the wedge that this would put between him and his best friend.

My fingers, numb and clumsy, fumbled for my phone.

Quinn.

She answered on the second ring. "Hey, Lo, what's—"

I opened my mouth, but all that came out was a sound. A broken, strangled sob that didn't even sound like me.

"Sloane? Oh my god, Lo, what happened? Where are you? Are you okay?"

I tried to breathe, but my chest wouldn't work. I stared at the whiskey bottle on the seat next to me, the label blurry through my tears.

"He's..." I whispered, the words cracking, sharp and jagged. "He's married, Quinn. Ash is fucking married!"

There was a long silence. A silence that was *too* long. The realization struck me. "You knew," I whispered, the words a fresh betrayal, a new knife twisting. "Oh my god...You *fucking knew.*"

"Sloane, stop," Quinn said, her voice frantic, pleading. "It's not that simple. I was trying to tell you. Where are you? I'm coming to get you *right now.* Send me your location."

"You *fucking knew* and you let me!" I screamed, the rage exploding again, hotter this time, aimed at Quinn. "You let me go see him last night! You let me sleep with him! You—"

"Sloane, listen to me!" she yelled, trying to cut through my spiral. "I couldn't just—"

"You let me make a fool of myself! You're just like him! You—"

"It's Kassidy, Lo!"

The words ripped through the phone, so loud they made my ears ring. I stopped, my breath frozen in my chest.

"What... what did you just say?"

"Sloane," Quinn's voice was shaking, half-sobbing now, an echo of my own broken state.

"I've been trying to tell you. Who he's married to. The reason I couldn't find the words. It's... it's Kassidy."

The phone hit the floorboard, and I just stared at it. My mind couldn't keep up.

Kassidy.

The name rattled in my skull like a loose bullet. And then—I laughed.

God, I laughed so fucking hard it scared me. It clawed out of my throat like something feral, high-pitched and trembling, the sound of someone finally snapping after years of trying not to.

Tears streamed down my face, blurring the world into watercolor streaks. I hit the steering wheel, gasping, choking, laughing. "Of course," I wheezed. "Of course it's her."

I mean, trust is the prettiest way to destroy yourself.

The laughter turned to sobs. The sobs turned to silence.

And then I smiled.

Wide. Broken. Gone.

Because the only thing I knew in that twisted, hysterical moment of clarity— Ash Walker didn't wreck me this time. *He fucking finished me.*

The laughter came back—monstrous, uncontrollable, tortured.

It wasn't a break. It was an awakening.

The last thread holding me together snapped, and I felt myself—

The woman who loved him.

The woman who held out hope, even when I knew better.

The woman who would have blew the whole fuckin' world up for that sorry bastard.

That woman—long gone.

And all that remained is the wreck he created—and the unhinged, heartless, savage bitch he unleashed.

UNLEASHED Bonus Epilogue

The steering wheel was slick beneath my palms. I hated this parking lot. I hated the flat, gray monolith of the state penitentiary that towers over me like a tombstone. The air here doesn't move right—it's thin, recycled despair. You can taste the metal and regret.

And in the middle of it, I sit waiting for a ghost of my brother—*my boss*—who's about to walk out of that gate, and the entire city doesn't even realize it's holding its breath.

They think the Moretti name died when he got locked away. Like that would stop us. They think we folded. They think we forgot.

Idiots.

When the heavy steel door finally creaked open, the man who stepped through isn't the brother I grew up with. The one who used to sneak espresso in the mornings and tease me for reading poetry instead of profit ledgers. That version of Gionni Moretti is dead. The prison didn't kill him—it forged him.

Since he took over the family business, I have never feared anybody more in my life. Gionni didn't fuck around. And the things I've seen him do...things I wish more than anything I could unsee.

But Gionni moved differently now—slower, heavier, deliberate. Like every step has been measured, weighed, and sharpened. The sunlight glints off his cuffs, and for a moment, I swear even the guards flinched as he passed.

He's wearing the same suit he went in with—black, custom-tailored, old money in every stitch—but time and muscle have reshaped it. He's broader now. Harder. The kind of man who commands silence just by breathing.

He scans the lot once. His eyes find me instantly—he doesn't search. Gionni Moretti never searches.

He knows.

My heart skips, a reflex older than fear. I've loved and hated this man in equal measure my entire life.

He walks toward my little red Camaro—an insult to his taste, I know—but it was the fastest way to blend in. I half expect him to sneer, but his expression doesn't even flicker.

He slides into the passenger seat, the car dipping under his weight, and the air inside shifts. It's colder. Thicker.

He doesn't look at me. Just takes one long inhale through his nose—like he's testing the air of freedom—and exhales slowly, the sound low and disdainful. The silence that follows is heavier than the prison gates closing behind us.

"Drive," he says.

One word, low and jagged.

I pull out, my hands trembling on the wheel. Asphalt hums under the tires, and the penitentiary shrinks in the rearview mirror—but its shadow stretches miles ahead.

For a few minutes, there's nothing but the sound of the engine and my heartbeat.

"So..." I start, my voice too small. "What's the plan, Gio? Back to the house?"

He doesn't answer right away. His jaw flexes once. The scar under his left eye—one I don't remember—tugs faintly when he finally speaks.

"First," he says, eyes locked on the horizon, "I have some unfinished business to take care of. We have someone to deal with. Someone that cost me some time in there. Name's Ash Walker."

That hits me like a bullet.

I almost slam on the brakes.
I groaned, shaking my head.

"Gionni, no." My voice cracks. "Please. He's not worth it. You're out. It's over. So let it be over."

He turned his head slowly, and I felt temperature in the air drop. His stare cuts through me like he's dissecting weakness. His eyes used to be warm, sea-glass blue. Now they're winter skies—flat, endless, and cruel.

"Over?" he echoes, voice dry as bone. "You think anything's over, *sorellina*?"

"I think it should be." I whispered.

He scoffs—a humorless, hollow sound that makes my stomach twist.

"He cost me two extra years in that hellhole. Two years sitting in a cell while rats breathed next to me. Two years not running my own empire." He pauses, the faintest ghost of a grin on his lips. "You think that debt goes unpaid?"

"Gionni, listen to me—"

"No."
The word cuts through mine, cold and final.

He leans back, drapes his arm along the door, casual as sin. "You know what his biggest mistake was?"

I don't answer. I already know this tone. The one that used to come before blood.

"He talked," Gionni says, almost amused. "Talked too much. In his sleep. To himself. To his celly. And he told me everything I needed to know without him telling me anything at all."

"Gionni..."

He keeps going, his voice silk over steel. "He was so worried about my guys on the yard after he cost me that time that he never realized who was sleeping beneath him. I let him talk, Alessandra. Let him give every detail to that celly of his—every weakness, every secret, every confession, every name."

My throat tightens. "You didn't—"

"Oh, I did," he says, smiling now, slow and feral. "And here's the kicker: my right hand got out a month ago."

I grip the wheel tighter. "No..."

"He's already in Walker's hometown. He's breathing his air. Watching his girl. Maybe already fucked her." his voice trailed off leaving the rest to the imagination.

My pulse hammered. "Gionni, please—don't drag her into this. She's innocent."

He laughs, low and quiet, like he's telling a secret to himself. "Innocence doesn't survive in our world, Alessa. It's a luxury for people who've never had to earn their power."

I want to scream, but all that comes out is a whisper. "You're free. Don't fuckin' ruin that."

He turns to me again, eyes narrowing. "Free?" He repeats the word like it tastes wrong. "You think I'm free because they opened a gate?"

The silence stretches, taut as piano wire.

He runs a thumb over his knuckles—scars I've never seen before. "Freedom's not walking out of a cell. It's making sure no one ever puts you in one again."

The weight of his words sits heavy between us.

When we hit the city limits, the skyline rises ahead—our skyline.

The Moretti empire was carved into every glass tower and shadowed alley. Gianni's fingerprints are all over it, even after six years. The streets still whisper his name like a prayer and a warning.

"People think I'm dead," he murmurs. "They'll learn otherwise."

I swallow hard. "And what about the family?"

He smirks. "What about them?"

"Gionni... they're scared. Some of them have moved on. Some have—"

"Betrayed me?" he finishes. "Good. Gives me names to start with til I can get to Walker."

There's no rage in his voice—just a quiet certainty that chills me to the core.

He pulls out a cigarette, lights it with a flick of his lighter, and exhales smoke like confession. The smell is familiar—nostalgic in the worst way.

"I've been planning every step since the first night they locked me up," he says softly. "Every contact. Every deal. Every death."

The words hit like a verdict.

"Gionni, if you do this—if you start again—there's no coming back."

He looks at me then, really looks. "I never left, *sorellina.* I just let them think I did."

My chest aches. This is the brother I prayed for six years to come home—and now I almost wish he hadn't.

We drive in silence until the city lights blur into a smear of gold and gray. The old Moretti mansion waits on the outskirts—a relic of empire, surrounded by walls too high for innocence.

Gionni stares out the window, smoke curling from his lips, and for a heartbeat, I see something behind the armor—a flicker of exhaustion, maybe regret. But it's gone before I can name it.

"You know," he says quietly, "you kept the business alive better than anyone expected. Even me."

"I didn't do it for you," I mutter.

"No," he says, almost fond. "You did it because you had to. That's why I trust you."

I blink at him. "You... trust me?"

He smirks. "More than anyone else still breathing."

It's not comfort. It's a warning.

He leans forward, voice dropping. "Call Nico. Tell him the king's home."

"Gionni—"

"Do it."

I nod, pull out my phone, but my hands won't stop shaking. My reflection in the window looks like someone else—someone trapped between loyalty and dread.

He notices. "You're scared of me."

I swallow. "I'm scared *for* you."

Gionni studies me for a long time, then looks away. "That's worse."

The mansion gates open before us, iron creaking like an omen. The guards freeze when they see him step out—like statues remembering how to breathe.

He pauses by the car, the night pressing close around him. Then, in a voice softer than smoke, he says, “Welcome me home, Alessandra Serena Moretti.”

And I realize—it isn’t his homecoming.
It’s the beginning of a goddamn reckoning.

Because the man who walked out of that prison isn’t my brother, anymore.

He’s *Gionni Amadeo Moretti.*

And not even God can help anyone who ever wronged him.

Have you wondered why Ash has been such a mystery in this book the whole time?

Because you get his POV on everything in book two as the story continues!

STAY TUNED!

Acknowledgements

To my amazing husband, Nicolas Easley – the man who has listened to me rant, ramble, spiral, and obsess over Ash and Sloane for way longer than any sane human should. You're my rock, my safe place, and the most patient (and occasionally slightly confused) listener I could ask for.

To my oldest daughter, Lilyana Easley, who was devouring the story – until it pissed her off– and has since then heard every little idea and plot twist I've came up with. To my bonus daughter, Caty Behnke, who became just as invested and loved hearing what I had in store next. You girls' reactions, eye rolls, and occasional "Mom really?!?" kept me honest and laughing through it all.

To my bestest friend and biggest supporter in the whole wide world – Amber Miller. My number one Alpha Reader, constant cheerleader, and the ever-so-patient (but not really patient) voice who kept me going when I wanted to give up. (Because who was I to tell her no to another chapter.) Amber, you are the real MVP of this book – this is just as much yours as it is mine. I couldn't picture having done this without you!

Thank you to Brittanie Behnke, my other ride-or-die and Alpha Reader, throwing out ideas that found their way onto the pages, and reminding me to keep writing even when I wanted to throw the whole damn thing out the window. You helped shape this story in more ways than you'll ever know, and I'm endlessly grateful.

A huge thank you to my beta readers: Tina Melton, Nikki Mahaffey, Lauren Sinclair, Tami Fortag, and Brittany Moore. Your time, consistency, feedback, and excitement for this story mean more than words can say.

Special thanks to Katie Thompson for being more excited than I was and for featuring my book in your shop, The Grove at The Orchard with my first-ever book signing.

And to Jamie Thompson, the first bookstore owner to take a chance on me – and in an entirely different state, at that! Thank you for putting Wreck Me Again on the shelves of Gregory PopUp BookShop in South Dakota and making this dream feel real!

Also to my coworker Oriana, who has heard about my book since I started working with her and has been a huge support the whole way.

And of course, to the one who inspired me to write in the first place – Destiny Witt – this book wouldn't even exist without you. Thank you for believing in me and telling me to go for every bit of guidance along the way! Also for being the very first person to purchase my book!

Last but certainly not least, a huge shoutout to "Sloane" and "Ash," for being so vivid in my mind that they gave me no choice but to tell their story.

To everyone who loved, supported, and encouraged me through the plot rants, the rewrites, and the messy middle of it all – this book is for you– thank you.

About the Author

I'm a mother, wife, and full-time hopeless romantic with a weakness for love that breaks you.

By day, I'm a wedding officiant of Written in the Stars and the one-woman powerhouse behind Brit's Resin Temptation & Handmade Creations, that studies Psychology. By night, I'm the trashy romance author of the Sin&Spiral Saga.

Fierce, messy, and a little reckless – I write the haunting love stories I've lived and survived, and the ones that reach into the darkest parts of your soul: forbidden, star-crossed, and dangerously irresistible.

These stories are for you – the tempted, the triggered, the totally undone, and the completely unhinged. You'll come for the kink, but you'll stay for the wreckage.

Follow me on social media for book updates, sneak peeks, and maybe a few unhinged ramblings about addictive fictional men and women that'll wreck you in the sweetest way- Indepedent Author Brit Easley.

www.ingramcontent.com/pod-product-compliance
Lightning Source LLC
LaVergne TN
LVHW010640110826
845149LV00014B/2902

* 9 7 9 8 9 9 3 7 4 3 9 0 5 *